Praise for *Season*

'We all start out as fans, and whatever our football journey, it remains the crux of all we do. To be reminded so movingly of the power of supporting – both our teams and each other – is a treat. A beautiful novel about the beautiful game'
Jonathan Pearce

'A beautifully crafted and accomplished debut – an emotionally rich and formally fresh examination of masculinity and alienation that deserves a wide readership'
Michael Donkor, author of *Hold*

'A highly accomplished novel written with gut-wrenching, net-busting depth. It effortlessly captures the touching intergenerational bond of two loyal football supporters. Every word counts; everything means something. This is so much more than a novel for fans of the so-called 'beautiful game'; this is a winner of a story in every way that all kinds of readers will inhale and remember long after the final whistle. I loved it'
Ashley Hickson-Lovence, author of *Your Show*

'The world of professional football is usually a graveyard of literary aspiration, but Harrison has found a way of using the match-day experience as a prism through which to examine the lives of the people watching on from the stands. Well observed, neatly handled and full of good things'
D.J. Taylor

'An absorbing, beautifully written, constantly surprising novel. The description of events on the field, as the side battles relegation, is riveting and completely authentic – but what goes on in the minds of the two men is just as compelling. The insecurities of youth and the frailties of older age are expertly explored. Ultimately it is football's ability to provide a sense of purpose and belonging to very different people's lives that makes this a most heartwarming read'
Roger Hermiston, author of *Clough and Revie*

'This is a tale familiar to the many of us who enter into maddening relationships with our football club. But it is far more than that – it is about the relationships we strike with others who share the affliction. It is told beautifully and poignantly by the author'
Riath Al-Samarrai, chief sports feature writer, *Daily Mail*

'Harrison skilfully evokes the unique and valuable role football plays in so many lives. He captures how moments of sporting euphoria and heartbreak can briefly but beautifully blot out relationship, family and work fears, and the depths of anxiety, gratitude and delight that exist beyond male inarticulacy. A brilliant, original and necessary novel'
Nicolas Padamsee, author of *England is Mine*

'*Season* perfectly captures the comforting rituals of football for taciturn males, old and young. Ambitions are thwarted, lives are lonely, the centre forward fails to hold it up. Yet there's always the hope that a millionaire in yellow might produce something unexpected in the box to avert the threat of relegation. It's an unexpected three points away from home for Harrison'
Pete May, author of *Massive: The Miracle of Prague*

'A football novel like no other, *Season* is a love story – not romantic love, but love of team, of game. It's a love that grabs you young and can never be shaken…for better or for worse'
Guy Swindells, TalkSport

SEASON

George Harrison

Published in 2025
by Lightning
Imprint of Eye Books Ltd
29A Barrow Street
Much Wenlock
Shropshire
TF13 6EN

www.eye-books.com

ISBN: 9781785634147

Cover design by Ifan Bates and Emily Dinsmore
Typeset in Adobe Garamond Pro and Bebas Neue

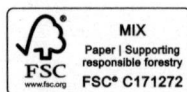

MIX
Paper | Supporting
responsible forestry
FSC
www.fsc.org
FSC® C171272

10 9 8 7 6 5 4 3 2 1

For Emily

SEASON TICKET

IT WAS A NEW SEASON, the first game since the last game, and the ground was busy well before kick-off. The Old Man arrived first, and he looked about for familiar faces as he shuffled crablike down the narrow aisle, double-checking the numbers daubed on seatbacks against the number on his printed ticket. Pop music came overloud from the speakers, pushing against the low hum of male chatter. The terrace was already filling up, and one or two men offered the Old Man a nod or some other greeting as a concession to the time they had already spent in one another's vicinity, years gone past. These were men for whom the rhythms of the year revolved not around meteorological or astrological systems; their days belonged instead to the football calendar, a capricious season all its own.

The Old Man had the same seat as last year, the same seat as always. This was the seat in which he had commiserated when they last went down and celebrated when they went back up, just a few seasons ago. The adjacent seat had been his wife's. Here, before the summer, they had watched their captain – the Finn, freshly recovered from his latest injury – tap in the goal that would keep them in the league. The Old Man had kissed his wife drily on the cheek as the Finn sprinted across to the dugout, where he was embraced by the manager and his coaching staff and the rest of the players, an unused substitute in a neon bib jumping upon his back. The younger men in the front few rows had surged towards the pitch, and after the game they had broken through the ranks of stewards in a tide of bright colour: garish jerseys flaring in the sun, scarves swinging like knitted flails. The Old Man smiled at the memory, looked to the seat beside his. The seat was folded back, yellow plastic stark against the dull concrete underfoot.

Throughout the previous season, the Old Man's wife had found it increasingly difficult to get to the ground and climb the steps and fight against the crowds. The stadium was too noisy, the tickets too expensive, and so this season she had resolved to follow the team from home. She had suggested, earlier in the summer, that he might do the same.

And how would I meet people then, he had said, as if he was always meeting people at the ground. What would I do with myself?

At the time, the Old Man had felt a measure of guilt, but it did not last. The football was important to him, now more than ever. So here he was, and there she was, and now the seat beside his was no longer hers.

Nearby, not far from that seat, the Young Man emerged from the concourse. That familiar climb up the steps and then the pitch – the grass impossibly green, the markings crisp and white and beautiful in the sunlight – opening like a huge flower beneath him. It took his breath away, every time. The hum of ambient talk welling all around, the loudness of the music, the stolid permanence of the goal in front of the terrace. Even the glare of the great digital scoreboard seemed like a blessing as it cycled through static adverts for cars and bookmakers and a local construction firm, the stills interspersed with highlights from the previous season. A clip of the Finn dropping into a knee-slide before the corner flag, teammates mobbing him after another late winner.

The Young Man arrived just as the players, the Finn among them, were coming out for their warm-ups. A shout went up from the back of the terrace, and many of the home fans stood. They clapped and cheered, their applause cascading down the steps and drowning out the music. These were the same fans who had viciously, almost gleefully, denigrated their own players for most of the previous season (right until the revival at the end, when the Finn came back – reborn, you might say – to save them). Nobody thought their enthusiastic support for the team, now, was inconsistent. Such was football, and such was the way of football fans.

Today it was the Englishman, their young full-back, who was first out, and he raised a palm to the terrace in acknowledgment of the men gathered there. Then the Finn, looking lean in one of the new training tops, and the Norwegian midfielder who had arrived on loan weeks before, heralded with almost hysterical excitement in the local newspaper. The Norwegian would never live up to his billing, the Old Man knew, but regardless, it was something to see him in the flesh. The Young

Man, being less cynical, had fallen for the hype, and he cheered as the Norwegian jogged languidly towards the centre circle. He already believed that the Norwegian would make all the difference this time round. He needed to believe, was what it was.

Soon the players began their warm-ups, and the fans settled once more into their seats, their conversations. The terrace was almost half-full, and more fans emerged from the concourse with every minute. The Young Man, looking for his new seat, moved down the aisle towards the Old Man, who stood and apologised for being in the way. The Young Man squeezed past and stopped at the seat which had been occupied in years before by the Old Man's wife. The Young Man nodded at the Old Man. It was his seat now.

The two men sat in their narrow seats, legs almost touching, and let the sounds of the stadium fill what little space there was between them. Down below, the goalkeeping coach was shouting instructions to his charges as he lined up a row of balls on the edge of the box. Both men let their gaze fall on the scene: the back-up keeper diving, pushing the coach's deliberately tame shot around the post. The first-choice keeper, the Dutchman, watched on, clapping his gloved hands in encouragement. The Old Man looked to the sky, which was pure and clean. Just a few clouds, strung in brilliant white threads against the blue.

Nice day for football, the Old Man said. There was a slight rasp to his voice.

The Young Man nodded. Football weather, he said. They'll be well up for it, a day like today. He looked over to the section of the adjacent stand which was reserved for away fans. They bring good numbers, this lot, he added.

The Old Man made a vague noise of agreement and looked across to where the away fans had started to gather. His eye was drawn to the flag moving in an unfelt breeze above the stand. He watched the flag whip and fall, the club crest contorting against a bold yellow background. It was impossible not to think, in that moment, of games gone by, of aborted cup runs and play-off finals and relegation six-pointers – decades of football and just the one real trophy to show for it. He had seen a lot in his time, the Old Man, and his wife had seen much of it with him. He had not given her much thought when he chose to renew his season ticket and go through it all once more, starting from nothing all over again. But now, for the first time, he realised what it would mean to do it on his own.

Down below, the goalkeeping coach had called in his players for a huddle. One of the fitness coaches was setting out a row of cones along the touchline. Unsupervised for the moment, a group of attacking players had gathered just outside the box, and now the players started taking shots into the empty net. A gull wheeled above the pitch, its shadow like a puppet on the turf.

When the home players were done with their warm-ups, they traipsed in twos and threes to the dugouts and disappeared down the tunnel. By now, the away fans were all in their corral. They were busy at work: some unfurling banners, others singing or taking photographs. When their players made for the tunnel, a fresh chorus started up in the away section. The Young Man looked over at them. The Old Man noticed him looking, but he couldn't think of anything to say. Then the Young Man asked if he could get past, since there was still time for a pint before kick-off.

The Young Man left the Old Man thinking once more of his wife. She would be turning on the TV around now, the Old Man knew. He could picture her in one of the two reclining chairs in the main room of their apartment, waiting for the games to start. He had sold their house and bought that apartment because he thought it would be freeing. They were nearer the train station now, so it would be easier to go on day trips to the coast. That requirement had seemed so important when they were looking, but they had not left the city once in all the months since they had moved. There were days now when they could not even bring themselves to descend in the lift and walk into town, and on those days they barely left that one room. But today was not one of those days – at least, not for the Old Man. It was something to be grateful for, he supposed.

The Young Man, as he made his way back down the aisle and towards the steps, heading for the concourse, thought also of his home, but only because he could not remember if he had locked the front door. He rented a ground-floor flat near the river, a street with willows draped verdantly across the water. Young people, like him, were to be seen paddle-boarding there on nice days. He lived alone.

The Young Man had to walk all the way through the city to get to the ground, and today two noteworthy occurrences had disturbed him on the walk. The first came as he was crossing the bridge at the end of his street, where a beggar asked him for money. The Young Man said he had no change, and the beggar, noting his jersey and scarf, told him to stop at the bridge on his way back and tell him the score. The second provocation came soon after, on the other side of the city, as the tide of men in yellow jerseys – all walking the same route – was thickening into a throng. That was when the Young Man had noticed a bird dead on the pavement, all opened up like a dropped sandwich. Now, in the concourse, the Young Man thought back to those images – the beggar and the dead bird – as he tasted his pint, and then he thought of the Finn. He hoped the Finn's ankle would hold throughout the season.

AWAY DAY

THE YOUNG MAN was at the stadium in good time. It was early, and a tentative sun lit the men, mostly, who were milling about beside a phalanx of coaches. The rest of the car park was empty.

The Young Man approached the nearest group and took up a position on the edge of the assembly. Two of the men shuffled to make room for him. A man in a beanie was talking loudly about the Finn – about his ankle, in particular. He said the Finn was becoming injury-prone in his old age, that fragility was a poor trait in a player who was supposed to be such a talisman. Nobody else was saying much; one or two sipped at coffees. The Young Man looked at his phone to check the time, then he put his phone back in his pocket. Then he took it out again. He had no new messages. The moon was still visible, like a projection, in the early morning sky.

Soon the doors hissed open, and the men and the few

women among them climbed aboard their designated coaches. There was an unaccountable smell about the Young Man's coach. It was his first away game, and he didn't know anyone. He sat beside a man older than himself and stretched out into the aisle when the coach started to move. The man beside him had a carrier bag by his feet, and from this bag he produced a four-pack of lager. He tore a can from the webbing and offered it wordlessly to the Young Man.

Thanks, said the Young Man, accepting the can. In return, he turned to the man and said, What do you think the score will be?

The man laughed – a bitter, joyless sound. Probably get battered, he said. But you never know.

The Young Man looked past him to the window. It did not occur to ask the man what he was doing here, making such a long and inconvenient journey, if he thought the team would get battered. Instead, the Young Man listened to the rumbling of the coach and the talk behind him – the same man going on about the Finn, still – and watched through the glass as a muted, faded version of the city drifted by, washed out in a film of dust. They drove past a man sleeping on a bench and, a moment later, a pair of teenagers dressed all in black. The Young Man's gaze lingered on the teenagers. Their colourless dress and their determined expressions and even the way they loped down the pavement made them look like they were up to no good. Coming back from a busy night or setting out into a busy day, perhaps. Either way, the Young Man recognised the type: lost boys whose lives as men had already been written. Finished with school, most likely. Fatherless, probably. Going nowhere, certainly. Then he shrugged his shoulders against the stiffness of the morning and stretched his neck, looking up at the sky. The moon was there, still, but in the rising light of the day it had turned sickly and pale.

The Young Man pulled out his phone again, but no messages had arrived since he last looked. He sighed and returned the phone to his pocket. There was a girl he was talking to: someone he had met through an app and who seemed different, interesting, in ways he did not yet understand. She said she lived on the edge of the city in a shared house full of strangers. She said she was studying for a master's degree with a loan she would probably never pay back. She said she wanted to do something creative with her life, but she hadn't settled on a medium and complained that, regardless, she had no impetus to create. They had not been talking long, but the Young Man thought her constant suspicion of the world and its intentions was strange in someone so young. He hoped they could keep talking. For now, however, it seemed she was either still asleep or had gone off him, as had happened in the past. It was not something he could control, but that did not stop him worrying about it.

At the back of the coach, the man in the beanie tried to start a chant, but it was too early in the day for most of the others. Nonetheless, some voices rose to join a watery and half-hearted ode to the Argentinian midfielder they had signed for next to nothing a few years earlier. (Some were saying, already, that the Argentinian was the best player ever to wear the shirt.) The Young Man looked over his shoulder, taking in the morning chorus. He had an image of the Argentinian firing in last year's goal of the season: a volley from all of thirty-five yards which had stunned the stadium into momentary silence. The Young

Man smiled at the chanting, at the memory, and sipped at his beer. He met the eye of the man beside him, but it seemed there was nothing worth saying.

•

Back in the city, the Old Man was waking up. He knew his wife, in the next room, would still be sleeping, so it was with care that he picked up his watch from the side table, stepped into his slippers, and made his way into the living room. The sun had seemed thick enough through his curtains, and now he was more alert, it registered that today was what they called a nice day. A good day for football, he thought, recalling his conversation with the Young Man, the previous weekend. Football weather.

The Old Man's balcony overlooked a construction site. As he blinked away the last of his sleep, he stood at the sliding door – as was his habit – to see what was happening down below. A few miniature figures, men in hi-vis jackets, busied themselves on the site. The great crane was still, however, and the townhouses appeared no more finished than they had the day before.

The construction work was behind schedule, the Old Man knew. He had read articles about the project in the local newspaper, and he remembered the spiel he and his wife had been given when they moved into the building. He could picture the houses rising into the space which had been made available for them, populating, at last, this new development in which he felt increasingly like the sole occupant. Increasingly isolated. It did not help that his wife was starting to turn in on herself, leaving him with ever more time to spend pacing the narrow balcony like a convict in a one-man exercise yard, shuffling prognoses and test results in his mind. Still, the incremental progress of the construction work was of great interest to the Old Man. He had joked with his wife, when they first moved in, that it was like having an additional television channel, but she was given only to complaining about the dust and the noise.

The Old Man got the door open and stepped onto the balcony, taking in the morning air. He liked it out here, even if his wife was right about the dust. It wasn't like normal dust so much as sand: an infinitely fine, reddish powder that settled on everything in the vicinity of the site and came back as soon as you brushed it away.

The Old Man ran his finger along the warm metal railing. He lifted it to see dust gathering in the relief of his print, the powder settling in those trenches that marked this hand as his, filling the whorls of his skin and erasing the lines to which no one else could ever lay claim. It made him think of a drought. Disasters on the other side of the world, entire countries in states of crisis.

Noises came now from his wife's room: the snap of a light switch and then a cough. They had shared a bedroom in their old house, holding out against inevitability for as long as they could. Now his wife finally had her own room. She blamed his snoring, but he knew she had long wanted it this way. At the first signs of her being awake, the Old Man stepped back inside. He slid shut the balcony door and locked it.

Morning, the Old Man called. He listened for a response from beyond the door of his wife's bedroom as he moved to the kettle. He turned on the kettle at the plug, and then he depressed the little switch to start it boiling. It was already filled with water from the previous day. He took down two mugs from the cupboard above him and set them on the side. Then he spooned a measure of instant coffee into each mug. The smell of powdered coffee rose to fill the kitchen. A tap ran on the other side of the wall.

While he was waiting for the water to cool, the Old Man lifted the sleeve of his shirt. Here a constellation of faded blue dots stood against his skin. He looked at these markings and let himself feel the full weight of the half-century which had passed since then. Here were the aborted beginnings of tattoos he had thought he wanted as a young man, each abandoned at the first touch of the needle. Three times he had steeled himself, each at a different parlour – as they were called then – and each time he had given up before anything larger than a pinhead had been scratched into him.

Days like today, the past pricked at him. Because today was a football day. The team was away up north this afternoon, and in years gone by, he would have been with them. Perhaps in another life, an alternate history, he might yet be on that coach, where he would be identifiable not only by his fingerprints and his singing voice but also by the ink rising in the form of an initialism, a crest, against the dry skin of his arm, proof of the one love nobody had ever asked him to quantify.

3

SIMULATION

THE TEAM WAS BACK in the city, and the two men were back in their adjacent seats. They called this place home: this twenty-thousand-seater stadium with its flaking paint and rusting beams. The men could be themselves here, watching in silence as the vast rotating screen cycled through the day's team sheets. The Norwegian was starting again, despite his poor performance in the first two games of the season. The Finn and the Argentinian and the young Englishman were all in the eleven, as expected. The weather was hot but cloudy: football weather, still.

The Dutchman, in goal, was finishing his warm-up. He took a moment to wave to the fans on the lower terrace, and then he made for the tunnel. The fans behind the goal clapped and started singing the Dutchman's name, syllables stretching, straining, to fit the tune of an old pop song. The Young Man liked the Dutchman; he was one of those players who fought for the shirt, who understood what the club meant to the people who lived here. And the Young Man thought of the Dutchman as a fatherly presence among younger teammates, a proud and dignified man – the sort who finished the things he started. He was far from the best goalkeeper in the league, but he was their goalkeeper. That was enough for the Young Man, who gestured now towards the Dutchman's retreating form.

He's going to have his work cut out this afternoon, the Young Man said.

The Old Man nodded without truly understanding what the Young Man was talking about. He was too preoccupied, today, to make conversation with his new neighbour. He had debated staying at home to be with his wife, but she had told him to go – and to make sure he was there in time for the warm-ups. She knew he liked watching the warm-ups; she had too, once, because it felt like value for money, squeezing extra entertainment from the ever more expensive tickets.

The Old Man thought of her now, letting his mind drift in the manner of the ragged clouds overhead. She had been bad that morning. What had he been thinking, she wanted to know, painting the bloody walls while she was asleep? She thought she had woken up in their old house; she had forgotten, for a moment or two, that they lived somewhere else now. Somewhere that was supposed to be more suited to them, with no stairs to navigate and a construction site beyond the balcony and a service charge which would rise year on year, every year, until they both died and the flat was sold.

The Young Man asked if he could get past. The Old Man looked up, surprised. From the look on the Young Man's face, he had asked more than once. There was still time, evidently, for one more before kick-off. One more journey along the concrete shelf, past the folded seats and into the concourse, where the bars were.

The Old Man had spent almost every other weekend, almost all his life, rooted to that same strip of cold, scuffed concrete. He had stood on this terrace, once; everyone had. But then football changed, and the club (est. 1902) had been forced to bolt seats to the ledges which rose, like a giant staircase, above the pitch. While part of the Old Man missed those days, he had reached the point now where he was simply grateful for somewhere to sit. In the coming years, as his knees crumbled and his hip pestled itself to dust, he supposed he would be more grateful still. And then – the familiar thought went – one day, he too would have to stop coming altogether.

For the Young Man, these worries were a long way off. He did not know, as he gently shouldered his way to the toilets, how lucky he was. And then he pushed open the door, entering a realm of concrete and porcelain, a space which smelled strongly of men. That urethral tang, the stench of sweat and kidneys, and the unselfconscious drumming of thick streams of piss against metal troughs.

When he was finished, the Young Man dried his hands at the sink, next to a man of a similar age with a young boy in tow. The boy was in full kit, the shirt and shorts and socks glowing pristine and unworn, fresh out of the bag. The father took care to make sure the boy washed and dried his hands properly, guiding him around the puddles on their way out. The boy even had shinpads on; the Young Man noticed this in the mirror, looking over his reflection's shoulder as father herded son from the bathroom.

When they were gone, the Young Man met the eyes of his reflection and wondered what it was that was so wrong with him. He had cut himself shaving that morning, and a flare of red, a thin scab, had risen on his chin. It looked like the start of a thread that, if pulled, would unravel his entire body, leaving only the clothes he had been wearing (club shirt, club scarf, chino shorts, black running shoes) on the disconcertingly wet floor and no further semblance of him to be seen anywhere.

The Young Man left the bathroom and made for the bar. He had to queue for a few minutes. When it was his turn, he asked for a pint, please. The girl who served him was probably studying at one of the universities in the city. She had her hair in a ponytail, and she was wearing a branded top and a lanyard about her neck to indicate that she worked for the club, if only in this limited capacity. She was pretty, he realised, and then he found himself wondering if she knew the girl he was still talking to – the girl who, it turned out, hadn't already gone off him after all. He touched his card to pay, and the barmaid smiled and told him to enjoy the match. As much as he was growing to hate his own job – the monotony of the same room and the same desk and the same computer – at least he didn't have to work weekends. At least he was granted that much: two days kept free for the football. The same, of course, could not be said for the barmaid, who bartered away her Saturday afternoons to serve men like him, each pint valued at around thirty minutes of her labour, her life.

As he drank, the Young Man scrolled back through various social feeds on his phone. Strange things were happening on the continent – something about a build-up of soldiers on a disputed border – and politicians from all over kept meeting to talk about what they would do about it, what might happen next. But the Young Man slipped past the news articles, lingering for a moment on a photo of a girl he had known from school who had been unpopular and undesirable then but was now, improbably, a mother to two children. He typed a different name into the search bar and landed on a familiar profile. He refreshed her feed in expectation of new information, hungry for morsels of her life.

So it was that while the Old Man, back in his seat, was thinking about his wife, the Young Man, in the concourse, also found himself thinking about a woman. He had messaged this girl – to whom he had been talking for weeks now – to say he was at the football, but she had not said anything in response. They were supposed to be seeing each other tomorrow. But signal was always patchy in the concourse and the WiFi never worked, so his feed wouldn't refresh and her message – if indeed she had sent one – wouldn't come through. This made him feel better about not having heard back from her, because this way he could imagine her reply had been sent minutes ago and was just stuck, for now, in an invisible backlog. The Young Man comforted himself with this thought as he sipped at his pint, which was valued, incidentally, at around twenty minutes of his own labour. It tasted like the bottom of the barrel.

When kick-off came, soon after the dregs, the Young Man was in better spirits. He had signal again, and still her message hadn't come through, but at least the game had started, so now he had this to distract him. The beer was probably working, too. And the sun was just coming out from behind a cloud, and the Old Man beside him was clapping vigorously every time their mighty yellows broke into the opposition third. The away fans, likewise, reacted with theatrical fervour whenever their team so much as threatened an attack.

The Norwegian was having another bad day in the centre of the park. Today he appeared especially flaky, misplacing passes and letting his opposite number – a squat, box-to-box bruiser – walk all over him. The fans were starting to get frustrated with the Norwegian, and the men on the terrace groaned as one when he hoofed the ball out wide, up and over the young Englishman's head and out for a throw-in. Twice more in the opening half he gave away possession, and twice the Dutchman rescued them when the opposition forward broke through, one on one. It was only because of the Dutchman's quick reflexes that they made it to the break without going behind. The whistle, when it finally came, was accompanied by a smattering of indifferent applause from the stands. The Young Man rose and went in for a half-time piss and another pint.

The deadlock seemed unbreakable in the second half, even after a flurry of substitutions and a change in formation. An Irish teenager made his debut off the bench, partnering the Finn up top, but the Irishman was feeding off scraps and the Finn seemed to have given up pressing. It meant the game was goalless, still, with ten minutes to go.

It was now, however, that the Argentinian, their wildcard, really came into his own. He was one of those players who grew into games; he seemed to become more dangerous in the dying stages of a match, relishing the exhaustion of the enemy. And now the fans cheered the Argentinian forward, applauding as he weaved through a forest of tired legs, daring someone to foul him. He pulled the ball close to his body, dropped a shoulder, and there it was – the inevitable lunge from a defender. There was barely any contact, but it was enough for the Argentinian to throw himself to the turf. He raised his arms, indignant, and looked up at the referee. The referee, seduced, blew for a free-kick just outside the box. The home crowd cheered, while the travelling fans cursed and booed, hurling a cacophony of abuse towards the pitch. You're not fit to referee, they sang. Who's the wanker in the black? they asked. Some of the men on the lower terrace gestured for the away fans to pipe down. On the pitch, meanwhile, the Norwegian had come over to start an argument about who ought to take the free-kick. The Young Man could see the Argentinian shaking his head, clasping the ball with jealous hands.

He had this confidence, the Argentinian. His South American flair was celebrated in these parts, even though his magic was often balanced out by what seemed like madness. Last season, for instance, he had picked up more red cards than any other player in the league. But the fans loved him too much to care, and the sporting director who had discovered him would spend the rest of his career basking in the Argentinian's glow.

Just over three years ago, before he was lured here (the powerful promise of English top-flight football), the Argentinian had been contracted for peanuts in the Spanish second division. He had no real fame; nobody in England knew who he was. But then an analyst here at the club dug deeper into his numbers. A scout was duly sent out to Spain to confirm his talent. The sporting director spoke to the Argentinian's agent, and in the following transfer window he arrived in England, a gem hidden no longer. The fans knew he was sure to be poached by a bigger club eventually, and they were determined to enjoy him while he was still here. Players like the Argentinian were plentiful enough in this division, but not in teams like theirs.

So the Argentinian took the free-kick; of course he did. And it was a peach, a worldie, the ball bending through time and space itself – or so it seemed – to elude the keeper and bulge the inside netting. The kind of goal that young people on social media would later describe as a sexy goal, a saucy finish. That really gets me going, the Young Man might say, adopting the pseudosexual language with which many young men engaged with the sport. Perhaps because they felt awkward using such language elsewhere and perhaps because it was all they knew.

But right there and right then, the Young Man had no room in his mind for anything besides pure, uncomplicated joy. The ground erupted with him, meaningless noise and four walls of spinning scarves and raised limbs: a scene like the salvation of some twenty-thousand desperate mendicants.

The Old Man, lost in the moment, turned to the Young Man and said, That's just what we needed, that. The Young Man smiled like his face had split. In the same instant, his phone vibrated in his pocket, and he was sure that he could feel in every individual pore of his bare arms all the places, all at once, where the sunlight was getting in.

4

HARD SHOULDER

The Old Man had seen many false dawns in his time, and soon it seemed that the previous week's victory, the Argentinian's late heroics, had been merely another. He was following today's game from home: he and his wife listening on the wireless, confined to their armchairs. When the third goal went in, she reached over and, with an arthritic hand, turned off the radio at the wall. The Old Man said nothing. He merely sighed and diverted his attention through the window to the construction works beyond the balcony. The international break was coming up, already, which meant finding distractions in lieu of club football. Today the huge crane was dangling a claw over the site; he could see it swaying slightly in the wind.

His wife coughed, and he looked over at her. She smiled, taut and quick, to say she was fine and that he didn't need to start his fussing. He was bothered about the football, but he knew she would not want to listen to him complaining about the game all afternoon. Another shocker for the Norwegian, according to the commentator. He had been directly responsible for at least two of the goals.

The Old Man rose slowly to his feet. Do you want a cup of tea? he asked. His wife nodded in response.

The Old Man turned on the kettle and dropped a teabag into each of their mugs. He looked out of the window as the bags steeped. A pair of gulls flew past at eye level, and he was struck for a moment by the strangeness of this sight, the newness of this perspective. Then he brought over his wife's mug and set it on the table beside her chair.

Would you mind if I put the wireless back on? he asked.

His wife said nothing. She was already asleep.

It was only natural that the Old Man should miss those days when he would have been down there, with the team. He had grown up in this city; he had been little more than a child when he first heard the roar of the stadium, first experienced the delirious press of victory and the impotent rage of defeat. And so it followed that he had crossed counties for the club in his teenage years: sometimes on his own, sometimes with friends, and sometimes with his father, from whom he had inherited his loyalty. Later, his love – and the club's brief period of real success – had taken him across national borders. Always, he had given his time and money to the club whenever it was asked of him, and he still had a couple of old shirts somewhere in the apartment that he had worn with the reverence of an acolyte, a true believer. On that night in Germany, the club's finest hour, he had been there. And the season before that European run, he had been there when they lifted the domestic cup – the one real piece of silverware the club had to show for itself. But that was decades ago. The glory days were passed, and what little warmth remained was an illusion, the last few coals glowing themselves out as he made ready for bed (a memory rising suddenly and unexpectedly from deep in his own history).

The Old Man considered switching the radio back on, but he did not want to wake his wife. And besides, at three-nil down the game was surely lost. So he entertained himself with the site below. He studied the workmen at their tasks as he sipped his tea. Soon he was asleep too.

•

On the south coast, scores of miles away, the Young Man had no such luxury of simply turning off the game, of dipping into unconsciousness. He was cornered in a hostile ground, waiting for the whistle to put him out of his misery. The atmosphere in the away end had burst with the third goal, and now there was a flatness to the whole affair. Even the home fans, as they celebrated the fourth, waving at the Young Man and the other travelling fans, seemed merely to be going through the motions. The Dutchman was on his knees down below, pounding the turf with a gloved hand. The Argentinian was watching from the other end of the pitch. He had his hands on his hips, a disinterested look about him, and he seemed only to come back to the moment when the manager shouted his name and made an indecipherable gesture.

The Young Man turned to the man beside him. Where does this leave us? he asked.

The stranger took a deep breath like he was thinking, and

then he exhaled. He was wearing a club jersey beneath an unzipped black hoodie, so he could cover up his allegiance in case there was trouble after the game. It was unlikely, but for some of the men, all the fun was in pretending.

I don't think we're bottom, the man said. He took out his phone. The lock screen was a photograph of a young girl with a gap-toothed grin – probably the man's daughter. The Young Man watched as he unlocked his phone and dismissed a notification without reading it. It saddened the Young Man, the way other people failed to realise their own good fortune.

Yeah, the stranger added, navigating to a live version of the league table. I think we're two from bottom if things stay as they are elsewhere.

Not exactly a great start, is it?

The man shook his head. We've been here before though, he said. Then his attention snagged on the events of the field. He cupped his hands around his mouth and shouted, Cunt! at one of the opposition players below. The Young Man smiled sadly. It would take hours to get home, and he had to be at work early tomorrow. His mother wanted to speak to him on the phone, as well, and he knew that would be a whole thing. Her news was rarely good.

The Argentinian had been enjoying a lively game, for his part, despite the scoreline. He was the one real positive. And now he picked up the ball in his own half and drove towards the opposition defenders. He parted a sea of red shirts, and even though the eventual shot was dragged past the post – the ball barely missing a photographer in his trench as it rebounded from a hoarding – at least the Argentinian gave the travelling fans something to get excited about. A few of them near the

Young Man perked up and started one of their well-worn songs. The Young Man joined in. They were singing about how shit this town was, how they wanted to go home.

When, at last, the whistle came, and the Young Man found himself back on the coach, he looked out of the window with sadness and frustration. On the way out of their designated car park they looped back on themselves and drove once more past the stadium: a draughty carbuncle, a tangle of squatting grey beams. The Young Man could not understand how the opposition fans had made a church of this place. And then the beaches, the grubby shreds of sand peopled by dog walkers who knew not to skip the stones without washing their hands afterwards. A seafront which was shit in the way that only former English seaside resorts can be shit. Losing here was an insult.

To make matters worse, the Young Man was dehydrated beneath the tang of beer, its taste metallic on his lips and in his mouth. He heard the man in the seat behind him mention the internationals coming up. It was probably for the best that there would be no game next weekend, the Young Man supposed, even though he would miss it. He was still seeing that girl, and he thought he might invite her round on Saturday. That was assuming, of course, that they could keep it going that long. She had said, already, that she did not know what she was looking for, that she was wary of getting into anything serious. The Young Man did not know if she was telling the truth or if she was trying to spare his feelings. He supposed he would find out soon enough.

He pressed his forehead against the window of the coach. At last, the motorway began to unspool beyond the glass. The bright orange of emergency phone boxes flared every now and then, and here a family of three had stopped in the hard shoulder: their car inert, the bonnet leering open.

The Young Man stared as the coach passed the stricken family. He needed a fraction of a second to process the scene – so shocking, to him, in both its unattainability and its mundane desperation. And as the coach juddered along, already miles away from the broken-down car, he seemed to speed past that image repeatedly: motorway markings slipping beneath the window, hazard lights flashing across his memories. The humiliation of the team's defeat fused painfully with the image of the father, mobile phone in hand, comforting his crying son. And he was sure there was a physiological symmetry between the fourth goal – the curve of the ball and the Dutchman's inelegant dive – and the visible distress of the mother. He could see her frozen in his mind: her body bent awkwardly over the front seat, the door yawning open, as she looked in the glove compartment for food, water. Her knowing there was nothing in there but looking nonetheless, just so she could say to her child that she had checked again, and that whatever it was he wanted, he would just have to wait a little while longer until help came along.

5

ITS OWN KIND OF LOVE

THEY WERE DEEPER into September now, the first international break behind them, but the heat had gone nowhere. Summer seemed to start and finish later each year, the way the Old Man saw it. The Young Man, standing beside him, knew no different. He was wearing a cap to shade his eyes, and the Old Man wished he had brought his own. Instead, he raised a flat hand to his forehead and watched in the manner of a soldier stood at salute as the players lined up and shook hands. It was his own fault for forgetting.

The Young Man was eager for kick-off. After the barren fortnight of the break, he needed a distraction, a chance to lose himself in the narrative of the team – a collective story beyond him and beyond his control. He welcomed, then, the surge of noise all around him, the singing of the anthem which they claimed was the oldest in English football, older even than the club itself. The Young Man spread his arms and shouted the words, and for a moment he felt himself forgetting.

The girl he was seeing had confused him, was what it was. That morning she had sent a long message saying that she really liked him, honestly, but she was scared of getting into anything serious because she had been hurt before. She didn't want a relationship, she said. The Young Man did not know where that left them, but he had resolved to keep seeing her in the meantime, while they worked it out. While she changed her mind, perhaps. He had resolved, also, to try and enjoy today's game. On paper, this was a winnable fixture. But football, as the cliché goes, is not played on paper. It is played on grass.

The Finn had turned his ankle over the international break, and the team looked that much weaker without him. The attack was toothless in his absence, and the game got off to a frustrating start. Men and women threw curses into the still, stale air, and the away fans jeered with each wayward shot, each block on the edge of their box.

The Young Man looked over at the travelling fans: a mass of purple shirts and pale limbs – an assembly which seethed like a great pulsating bruise. The way they all knew what to say and when to say it made him think of a mycelium: that being made of other beings threaded together, one thing and yet many things at the same time, its thoughts the sum of its constituents' thoughts.

The Young Man looked back to the turf. He could feel the fabric of his jersey sticking to his body. He picked at his collar, which seemed suddenly tighter. Beside him, the Old Man wiped at his brow, and his finger came away slick. The heat had settled on the stadium hours before kick-off, and the four stands had trapped the hot air above the pitch. Now it was like being in a cauldron, and the vibrations of large bodies around him only made the Young Man sweat all the more. He looked across at the Old Man and offered a comment about the heat. This was safe territory, talking about the weather. Between that and the events on the pitch, it saved the men from being forced to talk about anything else, and yet it still let them share in each other's humanity. Talking meant airing out that loneliness that, like the heat, encroached from all sides and settled, if you let it.

I can't stand it when it's like this, the Old Man said. Not exactly football weather, is it?

No, said the Young Man, laughing. This is more like staying inside weather.

The man in front overheard their conversation and, with the ball out for a throw-in, turned to face them. He said, I wouldn't mind that climate change so much if it means we get more weather like this. The Old Man had no response, so he simply smiled and waited for the man in front to turn back to the game.

The opposition launched an attack from the throw-in, but it only amounted to a long shot, pure speculation. The Dutchman was equal to it, dropping to his knees and catching the ball cleanly between his gloves. The away fans applauded the effort. The home fans on the terrace started to sing their goalkeeper's name.

The Young Man was trying to concentrate on the action, but he couldn't stop thinking about her and what she had said. He understood that she might have had a bad experience before, but to him that seemed more like an argument to try again.

Unless he was the problem. He scratched again at his collar, trying to get past the feeling that his shirt was shrinking on him. He could feel wetness beneath the sleeves where he had been sweating. He hoped he did not smell; he hoped the Old Man could not smell him.

The heat seemed to be getting to the players as well, because now the game entered a lethargic phase. The opposition seemed happy to pass the ball around the midfield, and the home players pressed without industry or enthusiasm. It was a common criticism of the manager: a trendy German – never seen without his cap – whom they had imported after one season of success in his domestic top flight. His teams were good with the ball, but they did not know how to press.

After a sustained period of possession, the opposition worked the ball to the edge of the box. The ball came to their number nine, in space just outside the white paint, who turned and fired goalwards, surprising his teammates as well as the two centre-halves in yellow. There was a moment of silence, of fear, and then the ball sailed harmlessly over the bar. The fans on the terrace gave an ironic cheer. The opposing forward cast a disgusted look towards that jeering, hateful, anonymous mass before wiping his face on his shirt and trudging back into position for the goal kick. There was one of him, and there were thousands of them. Their numbers made them strong, gave them the right to single him out. That accountability was why he was paid so much.

That was when the Young Man noticed a flash of orange in the adjacent stand. It was a steward running up the steps, two at a time. An old woman had been knocked out by the heat, and now she was slumped in her seat with people standing on all sides, fanning at her with their programmes. Her husband, beside her, was still shouting for help even after the steward arrived with a bottle of water and a walkie talkie buzzing at his side.

The nature of the clamour changed in a second. It changed on the terrace, too. The Young Man hadn't been watching the pitch; he had been too absorbed in the drama of the adjacent stand. But the Dutchman had evidently kicked the ball long, and the knockdown had been won, and now the Argentinian found himself through on goal. Barring the woman who had fainted, it seemed that every supporter was suddenly on their feet. Some twenty-thousand seatbacks clapped, a great drumming sound, and something close to silence settled over the congregation. It was a second or two before the net bulged and the ground erupted.

It all seemed to have happened in the same moment: the opposition keeper drawn to his knees and the Argentinian knocking the ball past him, much too quick to be stopped, before looking up once and shooting. He controlled the ball perfectly even at a sprint, like there were magnets in the ball and in his boots. The Young Man looked over as the Argentinian peeled away to celebrate, pumping his fists as he made for a corner flag on the opposite side of the field. The goal music started up, and now it was as if that same magnetism started pulling at the fans; men in the nearest stand came closer to the pitch, running down the steps and leaning over the hoardings. This player from the other side of the world seemed charged in such a way that arms, like filaments, were pulled to him in their thousands. Then his teammates caught up, and they were jumping all over him as the announcer said the Argentinian's name and the time of the goal. The away end went quiet.

Not far away, a second steward was bending down to speak to the old woman who had collapsed. She was conscious again. Her husband, the patron saint of uselessness, stood wringing his hands beside her. The Young Man, thinking of his fantasy team, turned to the Old Man and said, Did you see who got the assist?

I don't know, said the Old Man. It looked like one of their defenders touched it on the way through.

Right, said the Young Man. That was good play. I like to see us go more direct every now and then.

It was a good finish too, said the Old Man. He still had work to do from there.

He's magic, though. That's what he does.

Absolutely, said the Old Man. We've got to keep hold of him for as long as we can.

All along their row, all throughout the terrace and the other stands, the home fans were still on their feet, filling the stadium with their applause. Or is it more apt to describe this place as a cathedral? A place where concerns from the outside are ministered to and superseded. A hot place, today, of clammy hands on shoulders and the meaty smell of men who have been left out too long in the sun. Among them the Young Man and the Old Man, both surprised, on reflection, that they had turned instinctively to one another as the goal went in, compelled to share in the celebration rather than keeping it to themselves.

The Young Man watched as the Old Man lowered himself slowly back into his seat. His hands were threaded through with tracts of blue, the veins drawn out by the sun. A web rising prominently against the skin in a manner almost serpentine. Like the thinking strands of mycelium, perhaps. The Young Man looked back to the pitch, where play was about to restart. He pulled his cap down against the glare and prayed without words that their fragile lead would hold.

6

NORWEGIAN WINTER

THE YOUNG WOMAN perched on the Young Man's bed with her sleeve about her shoulder. She had wanted him to see the places where she had cut herself, obscure hashes in parallel tracks beneath the peach fuzz. The scars had long faded to white threads, and it was only with the overhead light that he could see them, the echoes of a pain she had felt as a teenager and had tried to gouge from herself.

He was not at the game today because she had been insistent about coming over. The team was playing away from home; he had paid for a ticket weeks ago, but it was easy enough to sell it to a man he knew from work – a fellow devotee. People were saying on social media that the Norwegian was finally going to be dropped today. There were younger players on the bench who could do a better job and who were permanently contracted to the club. But the team sheets would come later.

For now, he was with her.

I just wanted you to know, she said. Things were really bad for a while.

Right, he said, although he didn't really know what was the correct thing to say.

There was a man in my life when I was fifteen, she said. It was a bad time. Anyway, it's just so you know what you're dealing with, before things go any further. This is part of it, why I didn't want to go through it all again. I won't blame you if you back out now.

No, he said. Not at all. In the quiet, a fly banged itself against the window. Then, Does it hurt?

Not any more, she said. It did at the time, obviously.

She let her words sit. Outside, a car passed in a smear of sound, and then the quiet came back.

I did it in the bath, she said. With a razor.

I see, he said. It wasn't clear what more there was to say, although he was glad he was here, with her, rather than on a coach, travelling to the game.

Can I touch them? he asked.

Sure.

He ran a finger down her arm. Then he looked into her eyes. Her expression was open, expectant. It was upsetting, what she was showing him. He was trying to hide how he truly felt about the scars, but something must have registered on his face.

Yeah, she said. It was a bad time, like I said. I don't do that any more.

Good.

I mean, I haven't done anything like that since I was a kid.

Good, he said, and then she was crying. She was on his bed,

and she was crying, and he was supposed to be at the football, but he was here instead, pulling her body close to his, feeling the wet heat of her tears on his chest. It was difficult for him to know what he truly felt in that moment. It seemed they had both grown up in an age in which self-mutilation was almost a rite of passage, and they had matured into a milieu in which it was natural to show off your scars like tattoos and then cry, immediately after, on the shoulder of the boy – a stranger, really – you showed them to. A car alarm started down the road, by the river, and in that moment, the normality of the world beyond felt like an insult, a choice.

•

On the other side of the city, the Old Man was reading the paper. He would not have recognised or understood the scene in the Young Man's bedroom even if it had been explained to him, so stark and distinct were the boundaries of his own reckoning. And had the Young Man glimpsed the apartment in which the Old Man sat, a quiet so remote and complete and comfortable looking, he would have been angry. Here was the normality that was so insulting. Here was the choice that other people made. They chose to ignore all that was wrong with the world unless it was thrust into their faces; they discounted all the sorrow they could not trace, all the heartbreak they could not count in tough, white ridges against pale skin. The Young Man had always chosen to ignore it too, but now she had forced him to see it. Now he would struggle to stop seeing it everywhere he went. But it was not something the Old Man would ever read about in his paper. That awareness was not for him.

Many column inches of the local newspaper were given over to the day's big match, the game the Young Man had been forced to miss. In the paper there were previews and op-eds and a colourful pull-out commemorating the history of the fixture. There was also a great deal of speculation about the Norwegian, and the Old Man read it all. Various writers offered their suggestions as to why he had failed, so far, to make his mark on the league. Some said he was still shaking off an injury from pre-season; some said he didn't fit the German's tactics; some said he was being let down by the players around him. He was supposedly worth tens of millions, the Norwegian, and the club to which he was contracted was one of the sleeping giants of continental football. The fans were supposed to be grateful that he had chosen to come here on loan, a stepping stone towards bigger and better things.

But the Old Man had seen it all before. He had seen it so many times that he was losing his capacity to be disappointed by anything. His wife was no different. What the Young Man might have mistaken for indifference, had he been permitted to see it, was actually more like exhaustion.

The Old Man's wife was sleeping, still, and he could hear her laboured breathing through the closed door to her bedroom. He looked up from his paper. The dust had settled again on the balcony outside, more residue from the construction works below. He sighed and turned the page, and he was presented with a wall of adverts. He turned the page again and read another match preview which said nothing he did not already know.

•

Later that afternoon, an hour before kick-off, it was announced that the Norwegian would be starting, as the Old Man had known he would.

7

SIX-POINTER

THE HEAT PERSISTED into the first week of October. There was no wind, no rain, no respite whatsoever, and soon it was too much for the Old Man. These days, the heat did strange things to him. He feared his brain was melting in his head; his thoughts became puddled and watery, and the effort of moving from one room to the next, even, left him feeling shelled and vulnerable. Perhaps he was unwell. Regardless, when Saturday came around, he had no choice but to stay home.

See him now, this Old Man, sliding open the door and stepping onto the balcony and standing with his hands on the railing, feeling the heat coming through his palms. Dexterous hands, once, which had spent the better part of a lifetime employed in the art of fixing things. He looked down on the site below: the dust and the disorder and the gleaming struts of the crane, the bright poles of the scaffold. A pit where homes would one day go.

The Old Man stood like that for a few minutes, surveying the site. He knew he ought to go back inside, where it was cooler, but he couldn't bring himself to move. He seemed to recall having stood in that exact position, those exact conditions, in another life. It was like a proto-memory: tiny grits of dust on his tongue and metal beneath his palms and the veins rising belligerently on the back of his hands, pathways like neural links among the black hairs and liver spots. The taste of iron came into his mouth, and he had to close his eyes for a moment and concentrate on his breathing. He opened his eyes, and a silent gull glided past, flying level with his balcony. He looked over his shoulder, into the apartment. His wife was drowsing in front of the television. When he looked back, he saw that all was still on the construction site below.

On days like today you could hear the stadium from anywhere in the city. The Old Man intended to sit just inside the sliding door and follow the game by the noise: the bubbling tide of shouts and songs. The Old Man knew those sounds. He could picture the action by the way the voices rolled and surged: louder and more unified when they were on the attack; quiet and discordant when they were defending; silent in the strange second or two before a goal. The Old Man looked at his watch, its small, scuffed face held by a worn leather strap. There was just over an hour until kick-off.

Normally, the Old Man would already be at the ground by now. It hurt to be missing a game. And his wife would be on at him, he supposed, about the cost of his season ticket. Not that they needed to worry too much about money any more – not after selling the home they had lived in for almost all their marriage, a home which had appreciated beyond belief while neither of them had been looking. It would simply do no good for him to go, feeling as he did, and so there would be an empty seat on the terrace today – space for the Young Man to stretch into, if he wanted.

•

The Young Man, in that moment, was not far from the ground. He was walking amid a slow procession of fans, making his way down the middle of a main road (closed on matchdays) in the shadow of the stadium. He had a certain way of walking, the Young Man. You had to watch closely to notice it, but he walked like he was picking his way through a minefield, always wary, mindful of the need to tread lightly and easily, limping slightly. He was looking at his phone, refreshing his feed in anticipation of team news, due any minute. When the clock in the corner of his screen ticked over into a new hour, he withdrew from the tide of bodies and stopped by a lamppost. Men and women and children moved past, spilling outwards from the core of the city towards the stadium, where they would mix with those who had been drawn in from the towns and villages in the surrounding countryside – plus a few international travellers who had inexplicably picked this club to support when they could have chosen any in the world. Almost all the fans were dressed in shirts the same as his or similar: echoes of former glories and nods to fallow years long passed, disappointments whose taste had faded to memory.

The Young Man's jersey was a replica of the strip which had become synonymous with the club's European Cup run. It was a relic from before his time; the Young Man had never actually seen his club competing for silverware, but he still thought of the club's historic achievements as his own. The club had lifted one domestic cup, which meant he had lifted one domestic cup. And he regarded none of his personal triumphs so fondly as that night in Germany, the following year, when the club had stunned one of the last of the truly giant continental sides, stealing a place in the semi-finals of a tournament in which they had no right to compete. It was all lore to him, but it still meant something. Not least because it was a reason to take pride in the shirt, a source of bragging rights for a city best known for being quietly brushed aside.

The Young Man was sweating into his jersey. The sun glared down, and there was no sign of a cloud anywhere, no prospect of relief. It was strange to have such heat in October, but the seasons were changing. The months had lost their old alignments; now everything was shifted out by a few weeks. It was the same every year, but it still took the country by surprise.

None of that mattered, though, because the team sheet was live on social media. The Finn was fit again; he had recovered from injury and returned to the eleven, not a moment too soon. The Norwegian, who had been so poor all season, was finally relegated to the bench. A young academy graduate was starting in his stead. All else was as expected.

The Young Man's phone buzzed just as he finished digesting the team sheet. It was a message from the girl he was seeing. Were they dating? He didn't really know what to call it any more. All he knew was that it had become very serious very quickly, and that neither of them had seemed able to do anything about it.

This was what the Young Man had wanted, and yet it made him uneasy, the way her name flashed on his screen. The knowledge that she had the power to kill this fragile thing they were growing and return him to how he had been before, erasing those painful gains they had already made. It was like being one-nil up away from home; he was winning, but the margin between joy and despair could not have been closer. At any moment, she could back out and force him to confront the possibility (never far from his awareness) that he was somehow missing what everyone else seemed to have. That he was impossible to be with, unworthy of love.

The Young Man took a breath. He recognised that he had let his thoughts get away from him, and yet he was powerless to stop them. It was important, in moments like these, to remind himself that being with her was better than the alternative, which was not being with her. And that was why he needed the football so badly. It was the most effective and most harmless distraction he had ever found, the best way of quieting – if only for ninety minutes – the worries that chased him through the rest of the week. Everyone else was the same, he supposed. Even if their problems were different. And perhaps everyone else was lonely, too, and unmoored – as he recognised he had been before her and perhaps still was.

I've just seen the line-up, her message read. Enjoy the match!

Thanks, he wrote. He felt himself calming down, his heart slowing. He added, as a separate message, Maybe I could take you to a game some time?

He waited for her to reply before he re-joined the flow of people heading for the stadium. Theirs was a small city, but it was a football city; the performance of the team had a pronounced effect on the mood of the people who lived there. And as with anywhere else, twenty-thousand people wearing the same colour and singing the same songs always felt like a lot more. In a football city, on a Saturday afternoon, no believer could ever be alone.

At last, the Young Man could feel himself relaxing. He was cheered by the line-up. The Norwegian had been a problem all season, and it was good that the German had finally found the courage to drop him. It augured well for the game ahead, he thought. They were playing fellow stragglers this week. It was early for it, but the talking heads in the studio were already calling it a six-pointer. Most of the fans were convinced that they would lose such a crucial fixture, because to do so would be typical of the club, but the Young Man was not so sure.

Today the Young Man did not deviate from his usual ritual: a quick couple in the concourse and then to his seat. But he was surprised when he came out and saw the seat beside his was unoccupied. The Old Man was usually in position a good hour or so before kick-off. He had joked before that he liked to get his money's worth. The Young Man wondered where he was, why his neighbour might be missing the game. But when kick-off came, once the song had been sung, it was easy for the Young Man to shift his focus to the pitch and lose himself in what was happening there.

It was only later, after the Finn had put the first goal in and once the celebrations had died down, that the Young Man found himself looking again to the empty seat beside his. It seemed to him like a metaphor for something, but he wasn't sure what. He did not know that the Old Man, perched by the door to his balcony amid the hot air and the fine dust, was listening out for him, for all of them. And when the Old Man, dizzy from the heat, heard the surge of noise from the stadium – the swell of voices and the faint strains of the goal music that followed – he knew instinctively what had happened and how it had happened, and he allowed himself a small smile at the team's good fortune.

8

THE CASTLE

THEY WERE PLAYING away tomorrow, and the Young Man was looking forward to the game. It seemed a lot had happened since his last coach journey to a stadium in another city, even though it hadn't been that long at all.

The Young Man was thinking about the upcoming fixture as he stepped out of his building. From the doorstep he could see the willows by the river, trailing in the water's slow current. He had gone out without a coat, but he stopped on his doorstep and went back inside to get one – such was the changeability of that week's weather, the heat having broken at last. A moment later, he was back.

The Young Man turned up the collar of his jacket and set off down the street. It was cold and windy, and it felt as if autumn had arrived with greater vigour to compensate for its latecoming. The leaves had not yet turned, but the Young Man knew that every tree in the city would soon be aflame, russet torches everywhere he looked. He had visions of bright orange leaves, like sparks, twisting on the currents of the river.

There were no paddleboarders today, but as he approached the bridge the Young Man saw a couple in a canoe. He saw, also, the beggar who often greeted him as he passed on his way into town. Today the beggar said nothing; he was busy with his phone, and the Young Man crossed the bridge without a second look. The beggar was often to be seen sitting on a sheet of cardboard, an inert and dispelled magic carpet. This season might be his last, the Young Man knew, although there was very little that he could do about it. He walked on.

The Young Man was wearing a training top, official club merchandise. He often wore club apparel when he was not at work, and today he could feel the badge where its stitching rubbed at his chest. He saw, daily, simple renderings of that crest all over the city: mounted large on the outer surfaces of the stadium, stickered on the windows of parked cars, flying on flags outside pubs. He often saw it dyed into the skin of men who, like him, calibrated themselves to the rhythms of the club. Someone he knew from work – not a friend, more of an acquaintance – had the crest tattooed in full colour on his calf. The colours had wept over the years into a psychedelic smudge so that it looked, at a glance, as if this man was nursing a nightmare bruise on the back of his leg. But the man was happy with it. And where else could a grown man find that confidence, that sense of belonging?

There was nothing the Young Man had to do today, but he felt he needed a walk and some fresh air. The only person he wanted to see was out of the city, visiting friends. So he let his subconscious carry him, ignoring the faint suggestion of pain in his foot as best he could, and perhaps it was his thinking about the crest that led him to the castle. The Young Man looked up, taking in the boxy shape of the outer structure, the Bath stone.

The castle was Norman, a former gaol, and its true age was somewhat lost on the Young Man. His temporal sense was not fully rounded, and for him there was no point in making distinctions between the events of one hundred years ago and the events of one thousand. He was not like the Old Man, say, because he lacked the Old Man's acute awareness of passed time.

The castle was due for repair work, and blue hoardings had been duly erected around the lower walls. A crane lingered nearby, but nobody was working. The crane's arm, at a rakish tilt, seemed to present the highest point in the city. The Young Man looked up to the crane, and then he let his gaze fall back to the upper levels of the castle. The walls were crenelated at the top, jigsaw ridges whose purpose, for all he knew, had been lost to history. Or else they served some obscure function impossible to comprehend in this modern city of tattoo studios and vape emporiums and phone repair shops. He took a photo, out of habit more than inspiration, and walked on.

Tomorrow the Young Man would find himself standing among men and women like him, slapping an open palm against the rendering of the castle on his chest, the crest of the club he followed. He would not think about the castle, then, or about the history of his city. He would just be grateful that the English full-back, who looked to be the best of the club's young prospects, had found space enough to drive in a low cross and that the Finn, the club's all-time leading goalscorer, had been able to get his boot to it.

At the castle, back in the city, the repair work would continue in its slow and imperceptible way. The beggar would stand and watch the water passing beneath his bridge, and the boughs of the willows would move like drapes in the breeze. If you looked closely, as the Old Man had learned to look, you would notice the first filaments of amber and gold in the leaves, and this would compound your joy at the result from a difficult away game which really could have gone either way.

9

UNSEASONAL

THE YOUNG MAN AWOKE to a thin, gauzy light pushing through the curtains. He reached over to feel for the presence in bed beside him, but there was nobody there. A heavy, scraping noise had intruded upon his dream, and it seemed it was this which had awoken him. The noise continued now, the sound of something being dragged over his head, the locus of sound moving from one corner of the ceiling to another. This confused him for a moment, and then his confusion gave way to panic as he realised how late it must be, how his alarm had surely failed to go off before the sun could make itself felt through the fabric of his curtains. He felt a familiar dread – a dread he had started to associate with his work, so that even hearing the name of his employer made him feel tight-chested and panicky, like he was being constricted. And the scraping – a sound like a huge animal trying to bore a stone burrow – only added to the sense of unease, a subcutaneous, sickening horror.

It was only after reaching instinctively for his phone, after pulling away from sleep and letting the day break over him, that the Young Man realised he had neither missed his alarm nor made himself late for work. It was Saturday. There was no work today: only football. Even the noises, he realised, were perfectly accountable and benign.

It was the Young Man's upstairs neighbour: a woman in her thirties who said she worked as a mental health nurse. She had always made a lot of noise in her flat; it often sounded like she was dragging furniture across the room and then moving it all back again. The Young Man stared up at the ceiling and listened: the weighty scrape of a cabinet being moved, followed by the beat of footsteps, back and forth, and then silence. The quiet was unnerving in its own way, after the obscurity of the noise. But the Young Man was not surprised by his neighbour's disturbances any more; he remembered that she had been making noise as he went to sleep, and so it seemed only natural that she should be making noise as he woke up, as if she had been at it all through the night.

The Young Man eased himself out of bed and made his way to the bathroom. He walked slowly, gingerly. There was a pain in his left foot, a stabbing which came through the bone every time he set his foot down. This was a familiar pain, the legacy of a fracture and the subsequent immune disorder which had caused his body to turn on itself. His condition could not be cured but could be controlled by taking tablets for the rest of his life, lest parts of him began to crumble and his body broke down entirely. (His consultant had asked him, once, whether he planned to have a family any time soon, as the drugs had been known to cause defects in babies. The Young Man had only laughed.)

Pain like this was sharp in the moment, but it always faded to a dull throb when he relieved the pressure. The acuteness as he stepped lightly down the hall – the way his heart seemed to beat through the poorly fused bone – told the Young Man that it would probably rain later. Indeed, it was not long before the first droplets started coming down, beading his windows and making tiny, scattered impressions on the glassy surface of the river. It was more of a misting than a downpour, and it was like this all over the city, as if the clouds themselves wanted to give the fans a chance to make it to the shelter of the stadium before the rain started in earnest.

●

The Old Man noticed the early afternoon drizzle through his balcony doors. The forecasters had said it was not supposed to start until later, but their word meant little to the Old Man, and this was why. He looked at his watch and resolved to set off before it got worse. He lifted his coat from its stand and put on his shoes. Then he came back into the sitting room and made to kiss his wife on the cheek.

The Old Man's wife was in her chair. She did not get up to see him off; nor did she notice that he was wearing his outdoor shoes in the sitting room, which in earlier years had been expressly forbidden. There was a time, not long ago, when she would have been alert to such things. When she had been just as enthusiastic as him about the football. He remembered how she had loved getting dressed up for the games, how she had clapped every attack and cheered every tackle. She had once talked proudly of the players – her boys, as she called them – and harboured hopes for the future of the club. Now he wondered whether they would end up following the games in the anonymous sitting room of the same care home, whether nature might be kind enough to synchronise their deterioration so they might at least share the discomfort and indignity. Or was that worse? Would it be easier if he retained his health and wits, so that he could see more fastidiously to her wellbeing in the absence of any other kin or carer? Was there another world in which a grown-up child – a son, perhaps – would be dressing in the colours of the club and joining him at the game and helping to smooth over this final decade or so, another voice to nag at her to take things more seriously, for him to face head on what he could not avoid?

The Old Man pushed these thoughts from his mind. It was difficult to confront the reality of how much time had passed, how little was left. The barren years to come. His wife, when he went to kiss her, looked up at him with watery eyes and an inscrutable expression.

Good luck, she said. I hope they keep it going.

I doubt it, the Old Man said. But we'll see. And I'll see you later.

Bye then, she said.

Goodbye now.

The Old Man stepped into the communal hallway, which always seemed uncomfortably quiet, and locked the door to their apartment behind him. He was the only person in the lift, which didn't stop once on the way down to the ground floor. Here was the only evidence of human habitation: a set of dusty footprints in the foyer and a small cairn of parcels which had been left near the post-boxes for residents to collect. He so rarely saw anyone else in the building that he sometimes forgot it was not just them who lived there. But it was a new development, and not all the units had been completed – let alone sold. He trusted the building would feel more lived-in in time. Maybe it would even feel communal, one day.

The Old Man walked past the mound of unclaimed post and stepped out into the street, bending his head against the drizzle. As he walked towards the stadium, going as quickly as he could, he kept snatching glances at the sky. The rain was no heavier, but the clouds were darkening. They seemed thicker and more threatening every time he looked up.

Coming back might be a problem, he supposed, but he could always wait after the game for the rain to die down. At his age, he was well practised at sitting and waiting. It was only a problem for the lucky ones, in a way, and yet it was still frustrating. It was all his days had ultimately boiled down to, he realised: waiting, for all things and also for the final thing. And so his life had become a long and rambling sentence in which very little happened, an existence punctuated only by the matches every week or so as he waited for the period, the return to a split infinitive, to at last round the whole thing off.

But first there was the football. There would always be the football. And this week they had a good chance to extend their unbeaten run after a series of results nobody had dared to hope for and could still scarcely believe.

The Old Man and the Young Man arrived at the stadium at around the same time. The Old Man went straight to his seat, while the Young Man stayed in the concourse for a pint

– waiting for the rain to thicken, as he knew it would. Because although they were not long into autumn, the weather that day had a distinctly wintry feel. He would say as much to the Old Man in half an hour or so, when he finally settled in his seat.

The weather does this, now, the Old Man would respond. So many things were becoming unseasonal that the adjective was losing its meaning.

The players soon came out for their warm-ups, and beads of rain accumulated in their hair. After ten minutes, their shirts were sticking to their chests, and their socks were wet above their boots. Yet the fans were mostly sheltered, barring those in the very front rows. Another contrast, among many: the way the players were paid to sacrifice their physical comfort while the fans were encouraged to stay as warm and dry as they could.

The Young Man, sheltering in the concourse, was soon on his second pint, and having finished it, he forgot the pain in his foot. He felt happier now, better than he had all day. The Old Man, in his seat, was perfectly dry, and now he too was feeling better. The rain was only a problem when it turned into the heavy kind that drummed on the sheet-metal roof of the terrace. Then it could be annoying, if they were losing. But the Young Man didn't mind so long as he had his lager on the concourse, and the Old Man, who had seen so much worse in the course of his innumerable days, didn't mind so long as he did not have to think about anything other than the game.

10

OFFSIDE

THE YOUNG MAN HAD two tickets for the coming game. The match had been moved, at short notice, to Sunday so the fixture could be televised. Many of the fans had been annoyed at the rescheduling, but the Young Man didn't mind. It had made it easier, in fact, to get hold of the second ticket, the first he had ever bought for someone else.

Part of the problem was that the club, like its peers, was heavily dependent on TV revenue, which it needed to pay the wages of the players. If the club was relegated – as had nearly transpired last season – this revenue stream would be dammed, and the club would no longer be able to afford its wage bill. The best players would move on, and the parachute payments would be little consolation. There was, therefore, a great deal riding on their staying in the division, but this was always the case for all football clubs. The club was not special in this regard.

The Young Man thought Sunday's game would be a good one to take her to, not least because the capital wasn't so far to travel. He forwent his usual seat on the coach, and they took the train instead. The train was much more expensive, but it was quicker, and he supposed it would be more comfortable for her. It also meant she would not have to spend any time with the men who took the coach. This was a good thing, as far as the Young Man was concerned. The men on the coach could be loud and crass, and he wanted her to enjoy herself.

For her part, she seemed happy that they were going away together – even if it was not that far, in the scheme of things. The capital both scared and excited her (it was impossible to draw comparisons with the town where she had grown up), and she had already planned how they would spend their time after the game. She was looking forward to the match, of course, but for her, the trip held more appeal than just the football. Although she followed the fortunes of the club, she did so only in a detached way: checking the league tables now and then, listening in when more knowledgeable relatives and friends discussed recent results. Her greater interest was in the sights and tastes of the big city: the chance to ride the tube and eat dinner in a nice restaurant and pose for photos in front of the best-known landmarks.

They talked on the train up, looking into each other's eyes across the table they had colonised. They both had window seats. He asked after her family, and she said everyone was fine, thanks.

They've been asking when they're going to meet you, she added.

The Young Man laughed. You won't have that problem with me, he said.

Why not? She looked concerned. Are your parents not around?

I haven't seen my dad in years, he said.

And your mum? Do you not see her either?

He made an equivocal gesture and turned to the window. The flatlands slid past, endless in all directions. For the past half hour or so, this window had offered an unchanging view: a landscape of flooded fields and burst rivers. The standing water caught the light and glinted, knifelike, in the morning sun.

My mum lives on the other side of the country, he said. But I see her now and then.

You're not close?

Not really.

Why not?

You know, he said. The usual reasons.

She reached out and took his hand. He was surprised at her touch, as if he had forgotten how warm and vital her skin felt against his. He looked down at their hands, entwined now on the varnished surface of the table. Her nails were unpainted and bitten to the quick, lightly scabbed in some places where they had bled. But he could not keep his gaze from creeping up her arm. He was thinking about the scars hidden beneath the sleeves of her jumper. Like a cartographer of her body, he already knew all her features by heart. Even though he could not see them, he could have traced each scar through the fabric. He thought of them as strokes out of a runic script he could not read. Or else they were hyphens and dashes – conjoining long-ago notions of hatred and loss, the kind of darkness on which it is not healthy for a young mind to dwell. He wanted to make sure she never felt like doing that to herself again.

She might have noticed where he was looking, because now she affected a bright, carefree voice and said, Are you excited about the game?

He smiled, meeting her eyes. Always, he said. A bit nervous too, of course.

Why? Because I'm going to be there?

I always get nervous before a match.

Oh, she said. The rattling of the train, a rhythmic clicking, rose into the silence. Then, We're doing alright though, aren't we? In the table, I mean?

Yeah, he said. He liked how she referred to the team as we. We lost last week, he added, but we're still outside the relegation zone. It's early days, though. A few bad games and we're in trouble; a few good games, and suddenly we're mid-table.

Right, she said.

He was surprised that she knew even this much about the team and their position in the standings. But then it was difficult to live in their city without being aware of the club's undulations. There were always men wearing jerseys in the market, and the iconography of the club was often to be seen in the windows of pubs and shops. This was what made their city distinct from places like the capital, which was too big and too diffuse to ever be unified behind one badge and one shirt.

When they at last reached the terminus at the end of the line, they arrived to drab weather: drizzle, again. He took charge, guiding them through the station and patting, every few seconds, the pocket where he was keeping both their tickets. She laughed at this, saying he was like a dad at an airport, marshalling a family holiday, and then she started talking about the places she wanted to go after the game. He led her to the underground, letting her go first through the ticket barriers and watching as she inexpertly pushed her card against the reader. When they descended on the escalator, she stopped her eager chatter, and for the whole tube journey she was quiet and watchful. She seemed back to her usual self, however, by the time they surfaced and passed through the barriers on the other side.

It was a short walk to the stadium. He held an umbrella in one hand, and she took the other. He kept asking if she was getting wet, and he was strangely gratified when she pressed closer to him, leaning into his side. Every few seconds he glanced down at his own black running shoes, skirting the puddles which were forming in the pocked surface of the pavement. He had suggested that they both avoid wearing club colours, and as they walked the unfamiliar streets – past endlessly terraced houses and cafés with foreign-sounding names – he made a point of looking around for home fans.

We're behind enemy lines now, he said, only half joking. He had to raise his voice to make sure she heard him over the patter of rain on his umbrella.

But she did not seem fazed. She laughed and said, Will you look after me?

Of course, he said.

He squeezed her hand and repositioned the umbrella. He put it down only when they reached the turnstiles and entered the ground. The smell of rain was strong. They arrived amid a throng of fellow away fans, most of whom had been to a pub on the way. The Young Man recognised a face from the coach, but he did not linger to say hello. Instead he steered her up the steps, deeper into this unfamiliar ground, and guided her through the concourse to their seats. The weather was still miserable, but their section was mostly covered.

The rain, in this city which was not theirs, came down like a wet dust. It was as if someone had shaken out the sky, or else it was like being downwind of a great construction site with all those fine particulates drifting in a dampening haze. It made it difficult to see the markings at the far end of the pitch, but the Young Man knew the bright yellow of their jerseys would shine through the murk. When they came out to warm up, he pointed out their best players: the Finn, the young Englishman, the Argentinian.

Who's your favourite? she asked.

He thought for a moment. Probably the Argentinian, he said. He's the only player in this team who can produce real magic from nowhere.

She squinted down at the Argentinian's diminutive form on the pitch below. He was doing a passing drill with one of the coaches, taking one touch and then crisply returning each ball that came his way. Then she pointed to a player who was warming up by himself, jogging on the spot near the corner flag and seeming not to care that he was getting drenched.

I like the look of that one, she said. I think he's going to be my favourite.

The Young Man stared into the drizzle, following her finger all the way to the isolated figure of the Norwegian, who had finished his jog and was now stretching ostentatiously – spreading his legs and pivoting at the waist, touching each of his boots in turn. The rest of the players were running sprints or playing rondos in small groups. The Young Man laughed.

No way, he said. He can't be your favourite.

Why?

Because he's shit. And he's only here on loan. He's not even starting today, thank God.

I don't care, she said. He looks like a nice man. He's my favourite.

The Young Man scoffed, but because it was her, he let it go.

Just before kick-off, she produced from her bag a bright yellow scarf. Smiling, she looped the scarf around her neck, over her black jacket. Her hair was pulled back out of her face, and the pop of colour made her features seem even warmer. The Young Man told her she looked nice.

Thank you, she said.

Soon came the whistle, and for once, the Young Man did not stand and spread his arms and sing the club song as the team kicked off. He merely joined her in clapping politely after the few early attacks, each move culminating in harmless shots from distance, mere sighters. He noticed she did not shout or curse in the way that many of the fans around them were shouting and cursing. When the ball trickled out of play after a clumsy pass, a man nearby swore. The Young Man winced.

The thing was: the Young Man felt responsible for her happiness, since he had brought her here. And he realised now that it was important to him that she came to understand what he saw in this unfashionable and expensive pastime. He wanted her to get it the way he got it, to appreciate the appeal of standing in the cold and wet and watching eleven men in combat, in a physical chess game, against eleven other men. And then came a sudden thought of the Young Man's father.

The Young Man pictured a chess board, the pieces neatly centred in their starting positions with nobody sitting across from him, nobody to play against. The Young Man tore this shred of memory and, turning his attention back to the field, discarded it, letting it fall to the turf with the rain.

Soon the Argentinian, roaming in his untethered, effortless way, found himself in space down the right. The Young Man felt his fists clenching in anticipation, and she nudged him expectantly, sensing the move might lead to something. When the resulting chance was saved, she threw up her hands and shook her head. The Young Man hoped she might be getting into it. He kept asking if she was having a good time, and she kept saying she was, thank you. But even he had to admit, as the half wore on, that it was not a vintage game.

They were struggling to find a cutting edge, and so almost all their chances came from distance, and all were easily saved. She became insistent beside him that they needed to make a change at half-time. The Young Man explained that the German was unlikely to do that. It wasn't in his nature to change the team so early, and he was not the kind of man to do things outside of his nature. And as he was explaining these things, the Young Man realised, despite himself, that it felt good to be an authority on something. Even if she was indulging him, and if she didn't really care about his description of the new formation – which he thought was the key to freeing the Argentinian and unlocking his true potential in the number-ten position – what mattered was that she was willing to play along. That she was doing it for him only made him like her more. She soothed his need to belong and made him feel worthy of the people around him, the standards to which he held himself.

The two of them spent the interval in the unfamiliar concourse, pressed among wet bodies. Everyone was grateful to be out of the cold, if only for fifteen minutes. The Young Man's foot had started to ache again, the same pain he associated with changes in atmospheric pressure. His consultant insisted this was psychosomatic, but the Young Man was not so sure – and nor would he be.

The Young Man tried to ignore the pain as he lined up at the bar with his girlfriend, if that was what she was. He did not want anything to ruin this day. But then the teenaged bargirl, dressed in the merchandise of the rival club, told them she couldn't do black coffees, because the powdered milk came premixed in the cups.

Do you not have non-dairy milk? the girlfriend asked.

The bargirl shook her head in response. It's all premixed, she repeated.

Soon they were back in their seats: she with a green tea and he with a coffee. He had wanted a pint, really, but he had been embarrassed about ordering one in her presence. He came to regret it within minutes of the restart. They went a goal down almost from the kick-off, and then, as the home fans roared and the goalscorer launched into an embarrassingly choreographed celebration, the rain started coming slantwise, right into their stand. The Young Man kept looking over at his girlfriend, but he refrained from saying anything. The away fans were getting wet and cold and frustrated, and the atmosphere in their block was staring to sour. The man behind them was particularly incensed. He swore loudly when the ball went out of play. He said their French holding midfielder, a new signing making his belated debut, ought to fuck off back to where he came from. The Young Man looked at her again, wondering if she was grimacing because of the scoreline or the cold or because of a psychic discomfort which ran deeper than he could ever fathom. He could not bring himself to ask, now, whether she was still having fun.

The Young Man looked to the dugout, where a clutch of players had just returned from their touchline warm-ups. It was early for a change, but the German seemed to be responding to the frustrations of the fans. One of the substitute strikers, the Irishman, was pulling up a pair of yellow socks. The Norwegian was making ready as well.

When the board went up, she turned to him and said, I thought you said the manager didn't make early changes.

He never normally does, said the Young Man. Maybe he heard you.

Ha, she said. I doubt it.

The sky had darkened since half-time, a gloom settling over the stadium. The floodlights came on with the substitutes, and the light turned ethereal, something from a dream. It happened all at once, and then he could not help looking over at her and thinking how beautiful she was. And now there was almost something otherworldly about the pitch, the way the players' shadows poured from their boots in four directions, lit as they were from each corner of the ground. It was then, in the strange and unreal glow of the lights, that an opposition midfielder slipped on the slick grass. The ball was picked up by the Norwegian, his first touch since coming on. He passed it to the Argentinian, who played it out wide to the Kosovan, the club's fastest and strongest winger. The Kosovan dodged a challenge, hurdling the defender's outstretched leg like a knight

(L-shaped move in any direction, the only piece that can jump other pieces), and then it went back to the Norwegian, who played an uncharacteristic one-touch pass to the Finn. In a moment, their defence was split, and the Finn was through on goal. Everyone in the away section rose to their feet, and there came the sound of a thousand seatbacks clapping, a cascade of noise that rippled around their corner of the ground.

The home supporters went quiet, and then a shout came from the row behind the Young Man. Then he was shouting too, and so was she, and the ball went flying past the keeper and into the net in the same moment. The Young Man was stunned, just for a second or two, overcome with an emotion which he could not immediately identify but which, when he thought about it, revealed itself to be relief. In the jubilation that followed – scarves spinning in the air, broad grins and a kiss on the Young Man's cheek, lips cold with rainwater – nobody, barring the Norwegian, noticed the linesman with his flag raised, one arm rigid in the air and the bright panels of the flag shining like headlights through the rain.

11

UNSETTLED

There was discontent around the club, if the local paper was to be believed. Something was going on in that dressing room, and although it wasn't helpful to guess, everyone had ideas about what it might be. The disappointment of the last game had forced it all out, and now there were anonymous briefings in the press and rumours all over the internet. Someone on social media claimed to have inside information because his neighbour's uncle knew the kitman. He said there had been a shouting match between some of the players at the training ground after the last game. Two of the players had supposedly squared up, and the German had been forced to separate them. The promising run of form was well and truly over.

And some of the fans had started complaining, all of a sudden, about the poor atmosphere in the stands. A group of supporters was lobbying the club to let them bring a drum to the games. They said the team had been on a slump for years now; they said the club needed to do something radical to keep the fans happy and the team in the league. But the Young Man supposed this latest problem, whatever was happening in the dressing room, was not something that could be so easily fixed.

There had been talk in the stands, too, about the disjointed and inconsistent performances which had defined the first quarter of the season. At the last home game, the Young Man had turned to the Old Man and said they played sometimes as if they were eleven strangers who had only just been introduced to one another. Some of the men on the terrace were spending more than they could afford on the games. Nobody expected to win every week, but they wanted to see the players fight for the shirt. They wanted gladiators, was what it was.

On Friday it emerged that the recent discontent had its origins in one man. It was the Argentinian – the best technical footballer, they said, in the club's history. This was an opinion held by the Young Man and by many others his own age. The Old Man still insisted he had seen better, but those with memories of such length were few and becoming fewer. Not many of the fans recalled the glory days, relatively speaking. None of the younger ones had been there when ribbons in the club's garish colours were attached to the domestic cup; few remembered that team of mostly old-fashioned English bruisers who had taken the club to such heights, to the continent.

These days, the Old Man recognised very few of the faces in the stands. He barely even recognised the game: the speed of it and the way all the players were expected to dance with the ball now, even the centre-halves. The sport had changed so much in the past few decades. It had become a corporate, choreographed event, the fresh-faced pundits on TV banging on about expected goals and gegenpressing and wing-backs and God only knows what else. These days the heroes were all strangers; very few players were local to their clubs. They were mercenaries, mostly, the way the Old Man saw it.

Take the Argentinian, for example. The papers said he had become unsettled. There were bigger clubs, far away, whose representatives had expressed their intent to his agent. The winter transfer window would not open for two months yet, and the Argentinian was under contract for years more. But none of that meant anything to the man who made tens of thousands of pounds a week playing for the club. You might assume that so much money would have bought the Argentinian's loyalty, but the reality was that he could have made even more elsewhere. He didn't live in the city, because if he did, he wouldn't even be able to go to the supermarket without being mobbed for photographs. Instead, he lived with his young family in the countryside, on the border of the county. He was into his fourth season, but he still spoke most of his English through an interpreter. Few of the locals spoke Spanish. And now he wanted to leave.

·

The Young Man spent much of that Friday reading the reports online, while he was supposed to be working. He sent his girlfriend a message, and a link, asking if she had seen the news about the Argentinian.

Oh no! she wrote back. Isn't he your favourite?

Yes, the Young Man wrote. We'll miss him when he's gone.

But the Young Man suspected she did not really understand the depth of his loss, and he did not expect her to. Last night they had gone out for dinner, and she had said, only half joking, that he was like a child, sometimes, the way he talked about football. They had almost had their first argument about it. But in the end, he had given in and changed the subject, and he had let her talk about her master's degree and her demeaning new part-time job, which she already hated almost as much as he hated his own. He was aware now that the self-pity inspired by the Argentinian's behaviour was faintly pathetic. But what was so alarming was that he still couldn't help it.

The thing was, the Young Man sold his labour, and therefore himself, so he could pay the instalments on his season ticket and follow the football club all over the country. There were intermediaries involved in the following transaction, but you could say the Young Man worked longer hours than he wanted to – at a job duller and more unfulfilling than any he had ever hoped for himself – so he could pay the Argentinian's wages in return for lionising him. And he was one of the lucky ones; he could just about afford it. Because while the Young Man was not poor, he could recognise how expensive it had become to follow the team so closely. He had savings, yes, but his money had been hard earned, and he didn't want to dip into that pot before his time.

The Young Man had been looking forward to Saturday's game. It was a big-ticket fixture, a contest against the reigning champions. But the news about the Argentinian dampened his spirits. It felt like a personal slight. Like the best technical player in the club's history had turned his judgement on the Young Man, and the Young Man's inadequacies had contributed to his decision to leave. As such, the weekend was flayed of its appeal.

•

The Old Man read the news in print, in his apartment. He finished the leading article and set the paper on the floor. His wife looked over at him, and then she looked back to the television. There were inkstains on his fingers and a cheap, nasty residue on his palms. It seemed there was something malevolent about the whorls of his fingerprints, sea currents in black. The Old Man knew he ought to wash the ink away, but he was comfortable – an increasingly elusive sensation – and he didn't want to get out of his chair. He shared more of the Young Man's sentiments about the Argentinian and the coming fixture than he was likely to admit.

By now, at this point in the season, the two men had each formed a distinct impression of the other. They were only Saturday afternoon companions; their lives intersected only at the stadium and only on matchdays, and it was only on these occasions that they swapped their occasional comments about the weather and the football. They would not have thought of each other as friends. They did not even know each other's names. (Why would any man need to know another's name when 'mate' would do?) But already, life beyond the stadium had started to force its way into their conversations, and in these brief windows of time together each man had come to recognise aspects of himself reflected in the eyes and the speech and the mannerisms of the other. (Could the lonely recognise one another, the Young Man had privately wondered, even

– and perhaps especially – among a crowd?) And otherwise, they were alike, in that they shared a city and a crest and now a sadness at the Argentinian's sudden desire to leave. On a Saturday afternoon, that much was enough.

•

Come matchday, the Old Man was in his seat early, even for him. He waited for the players to emerge from the tunnel, and in the meantime he listened to the music piping through the speakers, watched the groundsmen wafting their forks at the pitch. A man wearing a club tracksuit and holding a clipboard walked behind the goal in front of the terrace. The Young Man, for his part, emerged only after the players had finished their warm-ups and returned to the dressing room. He made his way to his seat, and the Old Man stood so he could get past. The Old Man had been looking out for him.

Alright, said the Young Man, he who had never really known a man so many decades older.

Alright, said the Old Man. How have you been?

Fine, thanks. And you?

The Old Man shrugged. Oh, much the same, he said. And then he smiled, and for a second he appeared that much younger. I'll feel better if we win today, he added.

The Young Man laughed. He knew there was not much chance of that. He said, I guess it's been a while since you were here for a win.

Sod's Law, said the Old Man. The smile had already gone, the years returning with interest as he scratched at the back of his hand. The one game I'm not here and of course, it's the only game we win for weeks.

The Young Man smiled. That's what you get for picking and choosing, he said.

The Old Man laughed, but it was not a happy laugh. Perhaps he had failed to realise the Young Man was only joking. You'll see one day, said the Old Man. You won't be young forever.

The Old Man, beneath his familiar guardedness, seemed on the cusp of saying more. But what unsettled the Young Man was the dissatisfaction – a kind of anger, almost – behind the Old Man's words. He had hoped, the Young Man, that his own worries, his own inadequacies, were something he would grow out of. But the Old Man discomforted him because he was evidence that life did not work like that, that new worries would always come along, rushing into the space vacated by the old.

The men looked to the pitch for a moment, each in his own thoughts. Then the Young Man passed comment on the Argentinian. The Old Man hesitated, and then he said it seemed that the very character of their sport had changed over the course of his life.

Used to be you could go out into the city after work on a Friday and bump into some of the boys in the pub, he said. They used to have homes right in the city. I wouldn't even know where any of this lot live now.

It's a shame, the Young Man said, how things have changed.

Oh, said the Old Man. It's a shame, alright. More than you know.

Both men had already seen the team sheet for that afternoon. The Argentinian was not in the eleven, nor was he on the bench. They would struggle to match the champions without him. Worse still, both men knew there were bigger, richer clubs who wanted the Argentinian's signature, and both men knew a player as irreplaceable as him could not be expected – or, indeed, persuaded – to stay.

12

THE THINGS THEY WILL FORGIVE

IN THE CITY CENTRE, a cathedral. It had stood for some nine hundred years already, and in walking those cool flagstones – marked out like a vast chess board – any attentive visitor, even the Young Man, could feel the accumulation of all that time pressing down: all of it, all at once.

There were people buried in the cathedral grounds whose significance had long been lost – or else, their significance was lost upon the Young Man. But he liked the serenity of the cloisters, where schoolchildren often gathered around lanyarded adults, flashes of hi-vis amid the press of small bodies. And he liked to look up at the intricate stonework of the ceiling, the ornate ribs and the twisted accents. Faded paint in the knave, soft light pouring through stained glass. All this is to say that the Young Man knew well what it meant to be present in a cathedral. A place where the phone signal was always patchy through all those layers of stone and where it could be dark and light at the same time. Where you didn't have to believe to understand the place's significance for those who did.

By that definition, thought the Young Man, this place too, was a cathedral. The largest club football stadium in the country – a mecca, of sorts. A place where mendicants all dressed alike and brought with them their hymns and their tithes. A site of worship for not as long as the cathedral in the Young Man's city but for longer than anyone had been alive. It sounds like an exaggeration, but really it isn't.

The Young Man was in the away end, wearing a yellow track top and with a banded yellow and green scarf draped around his neck. At this stadium the visiting fans were kept high up and out of the way. It was difficult to make out the individual players as they flitted across the grass, so far below. From his heightened vantage point, the Young Man could see the men forming their rigid defensive lines: the German's favoured formation straining, almost buckling, under the home side's constant pressure. From here, it was only his distinct style of movement, his mannerisms with the ball at his feet, which distinguished one player from another.

Even though he was surrounded by visiting fans, the Young Man could only hear the din of the home supporters: a constant, bubbling surge of shouts, interspersed with fragments of songs. The Young Man had vowed not to be overawed by the occasion, but it was incredible being among such noise, witnessing football at such scale. Even his girlfriend had been impressed that he had a ticket to this game: a pre-ordained mauling on the other side of the country, playing away at the most famous stadium in the world against the most decorated club in England. She was impressed, and she was still not a football person in the same way he was.

As the game ticked over, so far beneath him, the Young Man's thoughts returned to the cathedral in his home city. He found himself re-living his last visit, just a few days previously, recalling the vivid primary colours of the stained glass and the cool feel of the cloister walls against his palms. The Young Man did not believe in God, but he supposed that in the football club he had found his secular equivalent. Perhaps it was easier to believe in something abstract – like a team, or an idea – than to believe in oneself. And that belief in the team held even now, even as the Dutchman was forced into a low save by the prima donna who captained the home team.

Seventy-thousand home fans groaned, all at once, and then their shouts dissolved into crackling applause. The shooter – an attacking midfielder like the Argentinian, only this man was the most famous player on the pitch, perhaps the most famous player in the league – clapped above his head to indicate his satisfaction with the rest of his team. Or perhaps he was telegraphing his pleasure at the fans, or even at his own talents and his sculpted good looks. He had long been known to be a playboy, this man, but recently, dark whispers had started to swirl in the newspapers. There were questions about his sexual conduct, suggestions he had mistreated young women and bought their silence afterwards. But the home fans didn't care. He was a demigod, here. In their eyes, he could do no wrong.

Ten minutes later, the first goal went in. It came from a corner, a looping header from their unmarked centre-half, and it sent the home fans into raptures. The Young Man swore in frustration. As far as he was concerned, set-piece goals were the worst to concede. He looked left and then right, and all around was a sea of people, all wearing the same blood-red replica kit, singing in one voice. Even through his discontent, the Young Man couldn't deny that this, too, was a spiritual place. The very history of their sport seemed suspended from the steel beams which were strung in a rigid webbing overhead. The rest of the away fans were gathered close about him, knotted together like so many outnumbered Spartans. He recognised faces from the coach, from games gone past, although none of these men were friends.

There was another similarity to the cathedral, the Young Man realised: he had no signal here either. He checked to see if his last message had sent, but it hadn't; there were too many phones, and nothing was getting through. It was just as well, because if he had seen that he had missed two calls from his mother, he might have worried. He turned his attention back to the pitch and tried to enjoy the game, but it was difficult when they were playing like this. They were missing that creative spark which, until so recently, had served to ignite the rest of the team. The Argentinian was still not in the squad. They had become too dependent on him, evidently, and they would continue to struggle in his absence.

The Young Man wondered whether the Old Man was watching the game on television, wondered what he made of all this. He had mentioned, last time out, that he had been to this stadium as an away fan himself. Many times, in fact. But that was long ago. Long before the Argentinian had arrived. Before the trophy drought which had afflicted the club for as long as the Young Man had been alive.

Did your wife not mind you travelling every week? the

Young Man had asked.

The Old Man shook his head. He smiled and said, She used to come with me, most weeks.

But now she doesn't even go to the home games any more?

No, not these days. She's not so well.

I'm sorry.

It's okay. We moved not long ago. Downsizing, I guess you'd call it. She was supposed to be happier in the new place, but I think it's making her worse. You know how things go. Well, maybe you don't. But still. The Old Man raised and then lowered his eyebrows. We're closer to the stadium now, at least. And the station.

There was a pause, then. It had been half-time, and the pitch was strangely devoid of life, the stands brimming with the low hum of private chatter. Then the Old Man, coming back to himself, had said, What about you? Have you got a woman in your life?

The Young Man had felt heat behind his cheeks. Yeah, he said, and he was surprised at his sudden urge towards candour, how he wanted to tell the Old Man all about his girlfriend and how they had met and how worried he was that she would discover that he was a fraud, not a real human being at all, and leave him. But all he said was, I have a girlfriend.

Good for you.

Thanks.

Any kids?

Who, me? The Young Man laughed, despite himself. No, not yet.

The Young Man had sensed that the Old Man, again, was about to say more, but in that moment the announcer had stated that the teams were ready in the tunnel. Both men had risen to their feet and applauded the re-emergence of the Finn, the rest of the players following behind him, and their conversation had gone no further.

But that had been last week, and now the Young Man shook off the memory and forced himself to concentrate on today's match, which was already threatening to get away from them. The home team had all of the ball, stroking it around the midfield. Their fans were cheering every pass, and the excitement reached a crescendo when a cross-field ball – straight and pure like the movement of a bishop (diagonal only, as many spaces as you like) – bewildered the young Englishman and found one of their wingers in acres of space, the perfect position to play it across the box, straight to the feet of their talismanic captain.

Then it was two, and the home congregation greeted this development with a massing of voices, seventy-thousand limbs raised skyward as the speakers flared into life. A million miles below, the goalscorer wheeled away to accept the adulation. A lot of the talk on social media, in the run up to the game, had been about this man, their star player. This millionaire who had just scored a tap-in, whose alleged victims were making themselves targets by speaking out, at last. It was big news in the nationals, but none of the local papers around here paid it any heed. In these parts, they said that first girl who had come forward was a liar and a slut.

The millionaire's name and number was announced, the time of the goal. The home fans roared. There might be a court case, but probably not. The stadium announcer did not mention the NDA this first woman had signed, and why would he? Nor did he mention the second and third women who had come forward, allegations dating from his time on the continent. It was rumoured that that there were even more women who wanted to talk to the papers, some looking for publicity and others for justice.

There was anger, now, in the away end. The Young Man looked at his phone, but he still had no signal. All he could hear was the home supporters; they were singing the millionaire's name with the tunelessness unique to football fans. When the Young Man closed his eyes, he was back again in the cathedral in the city. He could see candles burning: selfish hopes masquerading as votive offerings, desire rendered physical by pirouetting flames in the gloom of that architectural treasure. It sounds like an exaggeration, of course it does – but really it isn't.

13

SNOW

LATE NOVEMBER NOW, and the cold seemed to accumulate at the outer walls of the stadium, building up as sand builds against a groyne – a familiar sight in the lowlands, in the coastal towns an hour's drive from the city. The history of this place, in fact, includes that old story about refugees from the Low Countries, the strangers who came here in the sixteenth century to pray away the old continental constraints. They brought with them their stitching, and their canaries, and a wild, impossible knowledge of how to reclaim land from the sea. It was engineering, really, but it would have seemed like magic at the time. (To this day, the Dutch influence in the city has remained strong – but that is a different story.)

This, for now, is a story about the cold which had the Old Man clapping his hands not in praise but out of necessity, trying to beat some warmth into himself. His wife – lucid and pleasingly insistent, back to her old schoolmistress self – had demanded he wear his gloves if he was going to spend all afternoon standing around in the cold. The sounds of his clapping came, then, as a muted, impotent thudding. The sensation of wool on wool and the dullness of the noise reminded him of snow falling from rooftops, coming down in sheets... of snow slipping from the boughs of dead-looking trees, black trunks and brittle branches like an old woman's fingers.

The Young Man appeared just before kick-off, shuffling down the aisle, past men who had to stand to let him through. He passed each with thanks, a nod. The Old Man watched him approach and let him pass. Having finally made it to his seat, the Young Man turned to the Old Man, and their eyes met.

Alright, said the Old Man.

Alright, said the Young Man. He looked up at the sky, as solid and as quietly hostile as the surface of a frozen lake. When he exhaled, breath lingered in front of his face. Some weather we're having, he said.

You can say that again, said the Old Man.

The players all came out that day in their long sleeves. There was another change from the Old Man's day, when the players used to wear short sleeves even in January. It used to be that a player would get laughed at for so much as wearing gloves. Now some of them were bold enough to strut out of the tunnel with tights and headbands and all the rest of it. The Argentinian was like that. Had been like that, the Old Man reminded himself.

The club song soon started up, and the Young Man joined the throaty chorus. Then the singing dissolved into applause, and then a quiet fell on the terrace. The quiet of expectation. Of worry, if their form was anything to go by. The Young Man watched as they kicked off, keeping an eye on the Frenchman, the new holding midfielder, as he rushed out of position, trying to force an early attack. But he did not realise how much space he was leaving behind him, and when the attack broke down the opposition were able to break with a man over. They were lucky to get away with it in the end; the Dutchman, the only one for whom gloves were part of his kit, bailed them out, as he had so many times before.

The Young Man had been trying to immerse himself in the action, in the present, but now he got to thinking again. His last conversation with the Old Man came back to him: the Old Man asking, impossibly, whether he was a father. He realised that he had failed to ask about the Old Man's family and that perhaps he was supposed to have reciprocated. He knew very little about the Old Man's life, other than which team he supported and that he had a wife who had once shared his energy and enthusiasm for the club. When the ball next went out for a throw-in, the Young Man turned to the Old Man.

I was wondering, the Young Man said. Do you have children?

Play had not yet resumed, but the Old Man did not take his eyes from the pitch. He shook his head, cheeks red with the cold. Whatever well of volubility he had drawn from the other week seemed to have run dry.

So it's just the two of you, said the Young Man.

That's about the size of it, said the Old Man. Still he would not meet the Young Man's stare.

I see, said the Young Man, even though he did not.

The Young Man could not discount the possibility that he was scratching at a hidden tragedy, and so he did not press the Old Man further. He merely turned his attention back to the game and watched as the throw-in looped into their box. One of the centre-halves jumped for the ball, but his timing was off and the ball skimmed the top of his head. There followed a scramble just a few yards in front of the Dutchman's goal – nervous seconds in which the other centre-half hacked repeatedly at the ball, trying and failing to get rid of it – until the Englishman was finally able to intercede and hoof it clear. It looked to the Young Man as if they were in for another battering. It did not take long for his fears to be realised.

Soon they were one-nil down, again, and the outsized roar of the travelling fans seemed a defeat all in itself. The relegation zone loomed, and the Argentinian was still absent from the squad. The papers said he was refusing to play, trying to force a transfer. The Young Man swore for effect and shook his head. Some of the men around them were blaming the referee for failing to notice a supposed handball in the build-up, but the goal stood.

The Young Man felt the Old Man looking at him. He wondered if it was because he had sworn, and he felt strangely chastised. He considered apologising, but by then the Old Man was already looking back at the pitch, his eyes watering and his legs jigging for warmth.

It's a disgrace, the Young Man said at last. Honestly, what's the point of VAR if decisions like that aren't going to be overturned?

The Old Man shrugged. I don't know that there's any point at all, he said. He had started flexing his hands, trying to keep the cold out. But it was too late; the chill had already broken through the wool, burrowing beneath his skin. He might as well not have been wearing gloves, for how thin and ineffectual they were. His knuckles hurt already, and there was plenty more of the match left to endure.

Jeers came now from the away section. This was a side they really ought to beat, if they were going to stake a claim to this division. But the away players were up for it. They wanted it more. The home players – ridiculous and cowardly in their yellow – seemed to be elsewhere. They were lucky not to concede another by half-time.

The whistle was accompanied by a fresh surge of cold. It seemed to spill over the men in the stands, and the Young Man didn't emerge from the concourse until the whistle had blown again for the restart. The Old Man and the others in their row had to stand again so he could pass, but nobody seemed to mind. When the Young Man sat back down, the plastic seat was cold though his trousers.

No changes? he asked.

None, said the Old Man.

He never makes changes until it's too late, usually.

I've noticed that too.

The Young Man shook his head. The club seemed to be going downhill, but it was hard to gauge this sort of thing, week on week. With football clubs, things tended to change at a slow pace, barely perceptibly, until the team's fortunes soared or – more likely – slipped all at once, in the manner of snow from a sloped roof, a clifftop house into the hungry sea.

As the second half went on, both men noticed their breath gathering in thicker clouds before their lips. They were united, even if they did not know it, in their discomfort. The Young Man's foot had started to ache, and the Old Man could now feel the cold as a distinct pain buried in the pores of his face.

Either of them could have been elsewhere, with the women who mattered to them, but they had chosen to come to the game. It was important to them.

It was soon two-nil. With the second goal, the culpable defenders dropped variously to their knees or put their hands on their hips. The goalscorer sprinted away to the near left-side corner, where the away fans were gathered. He slid on the grass as his supporters surged forward, pulsing in red and white like a diseased organ. In the home stands, a few men were already standing up, gathering their things. The manager was yet to make a change, and of course, the Argentinian – the one player who might have been able to salvage something from the match – wasn't even on the bench. Their next best attacking option was the Irishman, the academy graduate whose league appearances had, thus far, been restricted to cameos. Defensively speaking, they had the Norwegian in reserve, but everyone knew how that would end.

It's a joke, the Young Man said. How soft was that?

I know, the Old Man said. But he was elsewhere. He was back in the snow, a rarity now. He was clapping, and his hands were sheathed in woollens, each one tied to his jacket. Another child was on a sled coming down the hill towards him. The whiteness was everywhere, like looking at the sun, and the aching purity of it made him want to shade his eyes. It hardly ever snowed these days, but it used to be that you could expect snow at Christmas. They used to have to shut the schools most every January. He could remember it like he was still there.

Did you say something? the Young Man asked.

What's that? said the Old Man, still seeing white. The pitch came gradually back into focus. No, he said. Sorry.

I'm going, said the Young Man. I'll see you next time.

On the bench, the Irishman, his fingers slow and silly with the cold, was trying to lace his boots. Meanwhile, the Norwegian's number was being keyed into the electronic board. There wasn't much game left, and already many of the fans had been driven back into the concourse, towards the warmth of pints and a piss and then the cold, again, of the walk home. This was the worst kind of cold, thought the Old Man, with no snow to show for it. He smiled sadly to himself and stood, once more, so the Young Man could pass.

14

THE LESSON

THE YOUNG MAN JOINED the press of bodies heading down the stairs. The stairwell was grey and industrial; sound bounced from every direction. The whistle had not long blown on their first away win in many weeks, and the men around him could not stop talking. They were heralding the performance to the rafters of this draughty old stadium, recounting the two goals and the incident which had reduced the opposition to ten men.

Today the German – unaccountably trendy in his club cap and oversized glasses – had tried something different, and today it had worked. He had torn up both the playbook and the team sheet; many of this season's ever-presents had been forced to watch, humiliated, from the bench. It seemed very out of character for the German to change so much in one go, and the Young Man had been surprised to see all those new names on the team sheet. It was particularly exciting that there had been so many young prospects among the eleven, all eager to prove themselves. Perhaps, the Young Man thought, it was time to re-evaluate what he thought he knew about the German's character.

Pundits often talked about how this was the best league in the world, and sometimes that kind of hyperbole motivated the younger players. Today, certainly, they had been all energy and enthusiasm. They played fearlessly, unheeding the expectations of the fans and the tens of millions of pounds the club stood to lose if they slipped (perhaps terminally) from the division. The old guard fidgeted on the bench – pulling at their oversized socks and going through the motions of desultory warm-ups on the touchline, at the German's insistence – as the academy graduates demonstrated how they ought to have approached the season from the very beginning. The Finn was one of the only veterans in the eleven, his status as club captain shielding him from any accusation of indifference. He took his early chance well, and the game was practically won when his rival captain, a slow and boxlike centre-half, earned his second yellow on the stroke of half-time. And then the ease with which the young Irishman had curled in the second, putting the game beyond doubt. This place is a shithole, the away fans had been singing. They wanted to go home.

Images of the match kept coming back to the Young Man. He imagined replays of the goals – particularly the second, the Irishman curling the ball again and again, the scenes of celebration vivid in his mind. It was almost compulsive, the way he made his brain play and replay those moments, viewing the same scene from angles behind the goal and off to the side and from above. The mental footage came washed in a shocking, bright technicolour, and the replays didn't stop as he trod gingerly down all those steps – taking care not to ask too much of his bad foot, heeding the complaints of his young and damaged body.

As well as the goals, he kept coming back to the sending off. He saw the referee drifting around the pitch like the spectre at the feast, a solitary figure in funereal black amid the blaze of coloured jerseys. The sole performer who had to always master his expressions, keeping his face and emotions level for ninety minutes plus stoppage time. A team of one.

The Young Man kept thinking about how the referee had been mobbed by players after the second bad challenge, how he had lingered, thinking, for a moment before reaching for the card in his back pocket. And then the schadenfreude of watching their captain pick himself off the floor and trudge towards the tunnel, chilled by the ignominy of an early bath. The square shoulders pulled back in an obvious approximation of pride, remembering at the last minute that he was still wearing his armband and turning back to the field of play to surrender it to a teammate. Then back down the tunnel, laughter bouncing from the walls as they closed in, batting away the approaches of backroom staff, coaches and tacticians and physios, as they tried to console him.

Cheerio, cheerio, cheerio, the away fans had started singing, the Young Man among them, waving at the centre-half as he disappeared, at last, down the tunnel. The home fans had whistled and jeered, hissed and spat, aiming their hatred at the referee. He was just doing his job, but his title had always been shorthand for isolation and unpopularity, the one person for whom football was not a team sport, a unifying or communal event.

Yet despite the buoyancy of the away fans, the jokes and songs as they made their way down the staircase – which kept cutting back on itself, as if it would never end – the Young Man said nothing. He kept to himself, descending amid a well of wild chatter, cushioned by the voices of those thousands with whom he shared membership of the football club. Claret paint ran in tramlines against the walls on either side. At these away games – when his girlfriend seemed to become distant emotionally as well as physically, slow to answer his messages, and without the stabilising presence of the Old Man in the seat beside him – he found it was easy to withdraw into himself. Today had been no different. Although that is not to say he wasn't pleased with the result. It was a good three points, by anyone's reckoning. The Old Man would have enjoyed that one; he was sure about that.

The Young Man rounded, at last, the final twist of the staircase. Ahead, a double door was propped open, a window to the cold. Police officers in bright jackets stood beyond, two rows of them lined up opposite one another like reluctant children at a school disco. There were horses, too. From atop his mount, an officer looked down at the Young Man as he passed. The officer had a baton in his belt, and the horse had a kind of headguard on, an echo from a less civilised age of gallantry, chivalry and unchecked disease.

The Young Man stared at the horse, transfixed by its air of strength and control. Then the creature's nostrils flared grotesquely, opening like twin portals to a place divorced from all conceptions of time and space. The Young Man could feel himself becoming unmoored in the black depths, all coherent thought lost to the darkness. The horse exhaled, and two spools of condensation rose, correspondingly, into the day – or what remained of it. Then someone bumped into the Young Man's back, and the spell, such as it had been, was broken. The Young Man gathered his thoughts, apologised to the men he was holding up, and moved on. The officer atop the horse remained impassive, although he followed the Young Man with his eyes. He seemed inured to the fear and fascination his mount evoked.

The police liked to keep the away fans from the home supporters. Where possible, they tried to funnel them through specific exits and then steer them across town to make sure there wouldn't be any trouble, although the warlike presence of the horses and the ready posture of the officers fuelled much of the trouble they were ostensibly trying to avoid. They were not particularly clever, these men in their starched uniforms, but they thought themselves superior to the rabble they shepherded from the ground. And in such a way, the travelling fans, the Young Man among them, were guided towards the car park where their coaches were idling. It was a long way home, although the win meant the journey would pass in greater comfort.

The Young Man accepted his place in that tide of bodies, almost all men. On every side they shuffled forwards and spoke in alternating boastful and martial tones about the game, about the next fixture. They tried to ignore the presence of the police. It was a happy day, although you would not have guessed it from the faces of the officers, nor from the expression worn by the Young Man.

As he walked, the Young Man looked at his phone. He had

messaged his girlfriend that morning to say it felt wrong to be going to the football on a day like today, but she said, after a lengthy delay, that he had paid for his ticket and so he might as well go. Staying at home and feeling sad won't change anything, she had written. The lesson was that you had to enjoy yourself while you were still alive. The Young Man supposed this was true, but it had still felt disrespectful, almost, to celebrate the goals, to give himself over to animal euphoria, in the wake of everything that had happened since the last game – a restless week that felt like so much longer.

He saw now that he had another message from his girlfriend, asking if he was alright. She cared about him, and he was grateful for her. He was ashamed, suddenly, that he had thought critically of her in any way. She might have resented him travelling, but it was only because she wanted to spend time with him at the weekends.

I'm doing okay, thanks, the Young Man wrote. The match was good. I'll let you know when I get home tonight. And then he was on the coach, and the engine was rocking somewhere beneath him. He looked for a while at social media, but almost every post in his feed was about the worsening situation on the continent. The troop build-up had not diminished; in fact, a border had finally been crossed, and the war which the experts were still insisting would never happen already seemed too far gone to stop. The Young Man plugged in his headphones, put his phone in his pocket, and closed his eyes. Soon they were moving. The men towards the back of the bus started up a song. He could hear their singing over his music: the soft rock albums his father had always liked. They were bands he remembered from his earliest childhood, those years when they had all been living together, in the same house.

The Young Man's thoughts changed like the tracks, one blending slickly into the next. He knew he would have to call his mother tomorrow to check on the arrangements and make sure she was okay. The usual things, after a death in the family. After his mother's dawning revelation that, having now lost both her parents, she was next on the list. But that could wait. For now, what mattered was that they were back out of the relegation zone, and they had succeeded in stealing three points they would probably need, come the end of the season.

It was a good game to have gone to, even though the Young Man was so far from home. He would always have this win; the lesson was that you had to enjoy days like these. And despite – or perhaps through – his guilt, the Young Man had enjoyed himself. It had been the right decision to go; it was okay that he had been so happy in the moments after the second goal that he had forgotten about everything else going on in his life, in the world. It did not matter that it was all coming back now, that against his eyelids he saw, again, the visage of the horse, nostrils tunnelling into its face, that mass of hot and living matter that would never know death the way humans did, would never appreciate the beauty of a first-half red card, so long as it was not one of your own who was trudging down the tunnel, shoulders back and eyes fixed forward against the humiliation, the awful oneness.

15

THE JETS AND WHAT THEY MEANT

THE WHOLE COUNTY was full of air bases. It had much to do with the region's geography: flat and off to the east with the continent only a hop away, barely any sea between the beaches of those coastal towns and the world beyond. World maps sometimes gave the impression that you could skip a stone from the eastern coast all the way to the Netherlands. But that is beside the point.

Because of the air bases, American jets were always tearing over the city. And even on quieter days, it seemed the chopping of rotors was a constant in the near distance. The Young Man's flat was on a flight path, and he often thought he could hear the opening strains of a thunderstorm when really it was just a jet. What with all the disquiet on the continent, it seemed that more planes were in the air, and they seemed louder than before.

Some commentators were already saying that the conflict would have profound effects throughout the world. Some claimed this was just the first rung on a ladder of mutual escalation towards death and disaster on an entirely novel scale. The Young Man was still not sure what exactly was happening and what the consequences might be. What few truths he could discern through the fog of war served only to confuse and upset him, and so he had resolved, earlier that week, that he would stop reading everything but the sporting news. The back pages held enough scandal and intrigue for him. For one thing, the league's poster boy, the superstar, the icon who had scored a tap-in past the Dutchman just a few weeks ago, had been beset by new allegations. More women had come forward, as expected. For the first time, there was even talk of extradition, but the Young Man knew that would be a long way off – if it ever happened at all.

Today was Sunday, another match rescheduled for television coverage. All that mattered to the Young Man was the football and his girlfriend, whom he would be meeting after the game. She seemed annoyed that she had to wait to see him, but he was not about to give up his season ticket and today he could not find a spare seat for sale anywhere near his own. He had already explained to her how going to the games was good for him; the football had a healing quality. And he could always see her after the whistle, supposing she had not entered one of her listless spells when she wanted to do nothing but steep, alone, in her dysphoria.

It had been a surprise to discover this side to her. For all her warnings, the Young Man had not anticipated the deep, lingering hurt implicit in her bad days, which were sparse and unpredictable and yet seemed to be becoming more frequent. She had said something recently about how being in another relationship was bringing back memories she had spent her entire adult life suppressing. He tended to leave her alone on those bad days, even though he was not certain whether she really meant it when she told him not to come over. (He did not know it at the time, but it had been written that children of the nuclear age had grown up with a diminished capacity for love.)

And she had told him, after all, that she had not been ready for this, and he did not want to give her an excuse to break it off now. He needed her; their good days were among his very best. And because of that, he recognised the value in giving her the space she needed to get better, to not ask questions whose answers he was not brave enough to hear.

Another jet came overhead as the Young Man was setting off for the stadium. A streak of man-made thunder, splitting the sky. The Young Man did not look up; instead, he focussed on the bridge at the end of his road. There he saw the beggar, looking out over the water. The beggar recognised him as he approached.

Enjoy the game, the beggar said.

Thanks, said the Young Man. You too, he almost added, as a reflex, but he caught himself just in time.

The Young Man knew they needed to pick up some form in time for the deep winter, when the fixtures were at their most congested. It would make the months of cold and darkness that much easier if they could string together some good results. And he had her, which helped; he hoped they would shelter one another, bring life to the shortest days. He crossed the bridge.

Here the willows trailed their skeletal fingers through the river. They were like children, the Young Man thought, playing with their hands in the frigid water. There were no paddleboarders this time of year, although geese were out in great numbers. The Young Man looked towards the fowl, massing on the banks. He might have noticed their presence, but more likely he was thinking about the game or about children splashing in the river or about how she had said – the two of them side by side in the bed she rented, staring up at the ceiling she rented in the room she rented – that she could never see herself as a parent.

Soon the Young Man was in the city centre. After the cut-through, he joined the throng of men heading for the stadium, the usual mass of yellow jerseys. The colour wasn't flattering, and some of the bigger men wore shirts which strained visibly against their forms. There were women, too, but it was mostly men. They all walked together and spoke across their groups about the team, the stadium looming ahead, listening in. Many of the fans had discovered a newfound optimism. The surge of goodwill all came down to the triumph of the academy players, the kids, the previous week. Almost overnight, the German had convinced the fans to believe in a way they hadn't believed all season. Things changed very quickly with football. The fans were capricious, and the Young Man was no different.

He looked around him now, conducting a semiconscious inventory of the crowd. These were his people, connected to him by the colours they wore and the songs whose lyrics they had memorised – some of them many decades ago. There were plenty of older men, as always at the football, but there was fresher blood in that crowd too. More children, the Young Man supposed, than an outsider might expect.

Football fans, when they became parents, tended to hand down membership of their club along with all the tangible things. And today there was no shortage of fathers with their sons. The Young Man knew that some of the children would have been at their first game, receiving today, without realising it, an inheritance that would define their Saturdays for years to come. Perhaps for the rest of their lives. And now he had noticed one family, the Young Man could not stop noticing the others; everywhere he looked, he saw small hands clasped in those of larger men. The father nearest to him was shepherding through the crowd a future season ticket holder dressed all in yellow and green: club shorts and an impossibly small and bright jersey with, presumably, the boy's surname and the number six on the back. The Young Man watched and listened, walking still, as the boy pestered his father to let him go into the club shop. The shop was visible off to the side, appended to the stadium and decorated with towering, blown-up banners depicting the Finn and the young Englishman and a woman of unknown nationality who played for the ladies' team. The banner featuring the Argentinian – arms folded, head cocked, cheeky grin – had already been taken down. The Irishman, with an expression that seemed to indicate surprise at his own good fortune, had gone up in his place.

Please, the boy was saying. Can we go in?

We went in just the other week, the father said, laughing.

Please?

The father sighed in mock exasperation. Okay, he said. But just to look. Not to buy anything.

The Young Man saw how the father rested a hand on the boy's head, how he always maintained at least one point of physical contact with his son.

Just to look, said the boy. I promise.

The father said something which the Young Man didn't catch, lost to the general swell of chatter. Then the father let his son guide them across the tide of bodies, among a crowd of supporters which parted, slowing imperceptibly, to let the child through, the father close behind. A second later, the gap the father and son had occupied was gone, more sons and daughters and fathers and one or two mothers rushing to fill the void, human particles moving like a liquid, the supporters adopting the shape of whatever space they occupied. The father and his son were already through the crowd, almost at the open doors of the club shop. In that moment, the Young Man could appreciate, for the first time, how absurd it was to bring life into the world. It was an act of faith, he supposed, now more than ever. But people did it all the same.

•

Not far away, on the lower section of the terrace, the Old Man (also childless) was already in his seat. Today he had been eager to leave his apartment as soon as he could. His wife had been watching the news all morning, and she seemed neither to mind nor notice that the headlines were on a fifteen-minute loop. She had watched the same bulletins four times an hour since she had woken up, and each time she passed comment as if it was all new to her.

He still did not know what he would do when she got worse.

Selling their house had freed up money for care, but he could not afford to pay indefinitely – and not for them both, if it came to it. And beneath all the attendant practical concerns, he could not work out whether all this would have been easier to navigate with adult children to assume some of the burden. Or would that only have made things more complicated? How would he have felt about wasting their inheritance on their parents' comfort – not least when no sum could ever change the fundamentals of the situation? As things were, he benefitted at least from a certain simplicity. There was no point leaving anything behind. There was nobody to give it to, and neither he nor his wife, as the saying went, would be able to take it with them.

It came as a relief to the Old Man that there was a match today; the distraction of the football made it easier to gain some distance from these cold and unpleasant thoughts. He was pleased to be here, in the stadium well before kick-off. He was content to watch the clouds passing overhead, the groundsmen feathering their forks at the turf, while he waited for the team to be announced. The activity around the ground interested him, salved his shame at not staying in the flat to keep an eye on his wife – no matter how vehemently she insisted she was fine. Here, at the stadium, he was home. There was always plenty to see before a match, none of it distressing or confusing, like the headlines which had blared all morning into the apartment. And it was so peaceful, before the place filled out. So quiet and expectant. Pregnant, almost.

The Young Man soon emerged from the concourse. He caught the Old Man's eye as he made his way over, and the two men shared a nod. The Young Man squeezed past and sat down. As usual, he surveyed the other stands before turning and looking behind him, briefly scanning the terrace for faces he might recognise. A well-dressed couple, obvious first-timers, were making their way up the steps, ascending towards him and the Old Man. They were looking perplexedly at their paper tickets, at the white capital letters sprayed onto the concrete, searching for a row which did not exist. It did not help that the numbers on the back of the seats had mostly faded to illegibility. They were obviously in the wrong place; this couple did not belong on the terrace. A moment or two passed, this silent comedy playing out before them, before the Young Man turned to the Old Man and said, Did you watch the game last week?

The Old Man shook his head. It wasn't on TV, he said. But I listened on the wireless.

Good, wasn't it?

Some result. I bet you were glad to be there.

Yeah, said the Young Man. Then, as he considered the reasons for the Old Man's absence, he began to wonder if it was cruel of him to talk about the away games, if he was somehow rubbing it in. He pressed a palm against the back of his neck, thinking, and then he simply said, We needed that. A fresh start.

The Old Man made a noise of affirmation. Then there was a quiet between the men, both watching as the smart couple approached the nearest steward. The man held up his tickets for the steward to inspect. A second passed before the steward pointed across the pitch to the stand behind the opposite goal, as far as possible from the terrace. The Young Man smiled. Then he looked back to the Old Man and said, So what's new?

Nothing really, said the Old Man with a shrug, a sad smile.

Not much changes for the better at my age.

The Young Man turned up the collar of his coat. He said, How have you been, I mean?

Oh, you know. Same old.

Is your wife okay?

The Old Man shrugged and said, We have good days and bad days. Then he turned to the Young Man and smiled. Were those embers of real warmth in his expression, something glowing in the creases which bunched at the corner of his eyes? Anyway, said the Old Man. How are you?

I'm good, thanks.

And what about your missus?

Yeah, she's good, thanks, said the Young Man. But that was the natural end of their conversation, and the Young Man was soon standing up, heading back into the concourse for a pint. He apologised as he squeezed past the Old Man, and the Old Man assured him it was fine.

Don't miss kick-off, the Old Man said, and both men laughed.

The Young Man didn't miss kick-off; he never did. Soon he was back in his seat with the taste of beer in his mouth, the stand almost full around them. A minute or two later, the players emerged from the tunnel. Combatants marching onto the turf in loose parallel lines, another young line-up for the yellows. There were handshakes, and then the players went bursting off in all directions, scattered to the corners of the pitch as the fans applauded. The Finn made his way to the centre circle for the coin toss. The Dutchman clapped the fans behind the far goal – the opposite side of the pitch, where the smart couple should have been. A minute later, the whistle blew.

The game got off to a scrappy start, and there was a flurry of yellow cards in the first fifteen minutes. The Old Man turned to the Young Man after the Irishman had been booked for pulling an opponent's shirt while chasing a long ball, a needless foul.

I wouldn't be surprised to see a red in this one as well, the Old Man said, the way they're going.

You might be right, said the Young Man. He thought, in that moment, that he could hear a storm in the distance. But the sky was not dark, and the air did not taste like it was about to rain. Nor had any been forecast today, and the Young Man felt none of the usual pain in his foot that might presage bad weather. And then the thunder came louder, and he realised it was a jet, flying over from one of the bases near the city. He took a breath and returned his attention to the game.

They said it was hard to love when you were bracing for impact. That was a line from a book the Young Man would read years from now. But what if you tried to quell your fears by not looking and not hearing, by distracting yourself with the game which was playing out before you, the away fans fired up by the big tackles and the home fans responding with jeers of their own? The Old Man said something, and the Young Man missed it beneath the noise, the first strains of the song which was swelling around them. The first half passed in this way; the interval passed on the concourse.

Then it was the second half, and before long the predictions of the men came true. It was the opposition's number nine who was sent off – the second game in a row in which their eleven had found themselves playing against ten.

When the applause, the laughter, had died down, the Old Man said he had seen that coming a mile off.

Didn't I tell you, he said. Didn't I say someone was going to get sent off?

The Old Man looked pleased with himself. But the Young Man said nothing, merely nodded. Despite his best efforts, he was thinking, still, about the jets, and what they meant.

16

OTHERWISE ENGAGED

THE YOUNG MAN MISSED the game that weekend because he had to travel for the funeral. He was on the train, refreshing the score, when he saw that they had gone one up. He smiled, despite himself. Arriving at the venue, an equaliser later, to tears and faces he had not seen for a long time. His mother's hug, much too tight. The way her make-up was loose around her eyes, the imbalance of her voice. The Young Man wished he could have been at the game, and then he felt bad for even thinking it.

17

STILL TIME

THE OLD MAN GRIPPED the balcony railing more tightly, though the cold metal burned his palms. He was looking down – had been looking down for longer than he realised – at the construction site below. Work seemed to have stopped for the year; there were no men in hi-vis jackets down there, and the cranes were still. No birds today, either, and the Old Man noted their absence with a sadness for which he could not easily account. The silence was total. After a few more minutes, the cold started to spread beyond the Old Man's palms, started coming though the fingers, tunnelling into the bones. It was like his marrow was freezing. He took his hands from the railing and, at last, went back inside.

The apartment was stuffy with artificial heat, and the Old Man's wife was sleeping in her chair. He knew he would have to wake her soon, but that could wait until after he had changed. It was a day for a thick jumper and gloves, black woollens to keep the heat in. Only the scarf he draped around his shoulders was in team colours. He had worn that same scarf decades ago, when they were playing midweek on the continent. He had held it aloft at the cup final, had lent it to her on the days when she was cold and had forgotten her own. He thought of it as his lucky scarf, but as he stroked the tassels he had to wonder: how much luck had it brought him, really?

As soon as the Old Man was swaddled in his warmest winter clothes, he started sweating in the heat of the apartment. Only his hands retained the chill of the outdoors, the cold to which he would soon return. He woke up his wife and told her where he was going, and then he told her again – just to make sure she would remember.

He looked at the table beside her chair and said, Where has your phone got to?

She waved a hand at nothing. It ran out of charge, she said.

Then let me charge it, he said. You need to have it on, don't you? In case you need me while I'm out.

The Old Man's wife did not address or even acknowledge his concerns. She just leaned forward in her chair and kissed his cheek.

Have a good time, she said. I hope they win.

And then the Old Man was out of the flat and alone in the communal corridor. Still, the smell of fresh paint and new carpets. The corridor was punctuated with identical, evenly spaced doors, with nothing to distinguish one from the other save the small brass numbers tacked above the peepholes. He made slowly for the lift. He could feel the cold in his hands still; it had been foolish to linger so long on the balcony, tearing up his thoughts and letting them fall like ragged confetti on the site below.

Even with his gloves on, it was difficult for the Old Man to properly flex his fingers. His hands did not feel like his own. As he pressed the call button for the lift, he wondered whether sensation would ever return. A few moments later, the ugly metal doors of the lift slid open, and the Old Man was surprised to see another man looking out at him: a fellow resident, a neighbour from the upper reaches of the building. The Old Man had never seen the stranger before. Nonetheless, he nodded, wished the stranger a good afternoon. The stranger nodded but said nothing. Such was the character of this new neighbourhood.

After passing the chain-link fences marking the perimeter of the construction site, the Old Man made for the river which wound through the city from one side to the other, kinked here and doubling back on itself there, tying together all the men of this place: old and young, past and future. A watchtower stood across from the meander, and a portion of the city wall, preserved even after all this time, loomed on the near bank. This path, which the Old Man was now following, led directly to the stadium. If he kept up the pace, the first grey struts would appear from behind the desirable riverside buildings in just a few minutes' time. As he walked, he passed people milling about beside benches, looking out at the water. Yellow jerseys over hooded jumpers, fans dressed for battle even though the teams hadn't been announced yet.

The path took the Old Man into the riverside development, a more built-up area. Here stood a cluster of shops and cafés, many with tinsel in their windows. One shopkeeper had stuck plastic snowflakes all over the inside of the glass. Closer to the ground was the pub, and here was a huge tree, without any decorations, standing proudly outside. The pub did a roaring trade on matchdays, the Old Man knew. Signs on the door proclaimed that only home fans were allowed in. As he passed, he heard a fragment of conversation, the bouncer chatting to a fat man in a smart shirt and a lanyard – the manager of the pub, the Old Man presumed.

On a decent run again, aren't they, the manager said.

The bouncer nodded. Might even stay up at this rate.

As the Old Man passed the tree, he remembered he still had to buy a gift for his wife. It wasn't clear what she wanted – or more accurately: there was nothing she wanted that he could provide for her. But she would still appreciate something to unwrap, he thought. It might even be fun to make something of Christmas this year. But he would not order a gift online, and so he would have to brave the city one day this week. Everywhere would be busy with shoppers, this time of year, and he was so easily frustrated by the crowds of tourists that gathered in gormless clots by the market. Just then, he felt a spasm of pain in his hands. He hoped it was a sign that his frozen nerves were returning to life, although it might have just been a response to the deepening cold, the bite in the wind.

At the stadium, beyond his designated gate, the Old Man held out his ticket and was waved through the turnstile. In the concourse, he considered buying a cup of Bovril or tea, something to warm his hands, but if he drank it then he would only end up needing to use the bathroom at half-time. He flexed his gloved fingers and looked at the nearest screen. It showed, live, the concluding quarter of another game in their league; a fellow relegation contender was drawing with a mid-table side. A couple of others were watching: a man and a woman, both wrapped in thick coats. The man had a hat on.

That result's not doing us any favours, the Old Man said.

The woman smiled at him and said, There's still time.

The Old Man nodded, then he looked away. He went to the bathroom while the ground was quiet, and then he was in his seat, waiting for the teams to be announced. A few away fans were already in their section, but most of the supporters were taking refuge in the relative warmth of the concourse. The Old Man could see his breath in front of his face. He tried to bend his fingers again, and this time he was almost able to make a fist before the pain became too much to bear.

The team, when it was announced, was much as expected. The Irishman was starting up front again, alongside the Finn. The eleven was among the youngest the club had ever fielded in the top flight, and when those academy lads emerged onto the chilled pitch they were all smiles, waving at the few hardy fans already shivering in their seats.

The Old Man folded his hands in his lap and watched the players warming up. There were many he didn't recognise, or whom he recognised only when they turned a certain way or dropped a shoulder or made to shoot into the empty net – signatures of their bodies, autographed postures. It would take time to learn the names and numbers of the academy players who were training and playing now with the first team. The Irishman, down below, was discernible from his gait. He wore a higher number, forty-something, the Old Man knew – a sign of the Irishman's formerly unimpressive position in the club hierarchy.

The Old Man watched the Irishman jogging between

cones, exchanging passes with the Finn, and he looked up only when the Young Man came to take the seat next to him. They exchanged their greetings, passed comment on the foulness of the weather, the proximity of Christmas and the club's flickering hopes of survival in the league. Then they sat together amid the growing commotion and waited for kick-off. Quiet settled, like the cold, on the moulded plastic of their seats, the pocked surface of the concrete beneath their shoes. The Old Man decided he had had enough silence for one day.

Are you not going back in for a pint?

The Young Man shook his head. Not today, he said.

The Old Man laughed. Are you feeling alright? Got a fever or something?

I'm fine, said the Young Man. I just don't feel like a drink.

What's the matter? Girl troubles?

What? The Young Man turned to the Old Man. What makes you say that?

No reason, said the Old Man. He smirked. Just remember what I was like when I was your age, is all.

The Young Man didn't respond. The terrace was now almost full, and the Old Man was able to tune into the chatter of the men behind him: talk about the Irishman not being good enough for this league, saying how one or two decent games didn't make him a quality player.

When the players came out of the tunnel, just fifteen minutes later, the Old Man looked out for the Irishman. He alone moved like he was encumbered, his slow, loping step unusual for an athlete. The other players all practically bounded out, floating above the turf as if they held total mastery over their bodies. The Old Man smiled sadly at their fleet-footedness, the sureness of their movement. The players were remote from him by virtue of their wealth and their fame and their distinction within their field, but nothing could have separated them from the Old Man more than their youth.

That was the thing with the young, the Old Man thought: they propelled themselves through the world with such confidence, barrelling everyone else out of the way. And they took it for granted. It occurred to none of them that a day would come when they would not move so freely and assuredly. He had been the same, once.

At this thought, the Old Man turned to the Young Man. They were both standing now, hailing the arrival of the team and absorbing the announcer's steady reading of the names and numbers of the players. In his mind, the Young Man was trying to assemble the team into a likely formation, shuffling numbers and positions and slotting each of the men into their places, predicting the German's schematics for the fixture.

You're lucky, you know, the Old Man said, raising his voice to make himself heard over the applause.

The Young Man looked over. A faint smile, no real annoyance at having his thoughts interrupted, banks of players scattering in his mind. What do you mean?

I just mean that you've got everything to come, said the Old Man. Try and slow down, son. Enjoy it.

Thank you, said the Young Man. I will.

Trust me, you'll have plenty of time to worry when you're older.

Right, said the Young Man.

The Old Man smiled. Then he turned back to the pitch and clapped his hands, a wool-on-wool thud. The Young Man was faintly bemused, but he was also grateful for the Old Man's concern. He joined in with the singing, and then the two men sat back down, anticipating the whistle. In those few empty seconds, the Old Man's thoughts floated – more confetti – out over the terrace, beyond the ground. His worries landed on the river, where the current carried them towards his apartment. He supposed his wife would be sleeping in her armchair with the radio on, tuned to coverage of the game. He considered what gift he might buy her for Christmas. And then he couldn't help but wonder – as he watched the twenty-two young men taking their positions below, as the river became choked with anxieties, paper saturating and turning to mulch – if she would remember to get him something in return.

18

ALLOWANCES

They were playing away on Boxing Day, and so the Old Man wouldn't be at the game. He planned to watch the coverage from his apartment instead. His wife wanted to watch it too. She had asked him to make sure she was awake for it.

The Old Man had been looking forward to the Boxing Day fixture more than he had been looking forward to Christmas. He hoped it might feel a bit like last season, when they had been playing at home on Boxing Day and he and his wife had gone together. The problem was that the team had changed so much in the past year that his wife would barely recognise any of the players. The Irishman was getting almost ninety minutes every game. The Argentinian was still nowhere to be seen; he was rumoured to be going any day now. Even the Finn had grown out his beard.

The Old Man knew he would spend much of the game

fielding questions about who was on the ball now and which one was that number forty-five, again? But it didn't matter. Not in the scheme of things. The Old Man looked at his watch. He set down the newspaper he had been trying to read – the same faces and voices on the sports pages – and ambled over to the balcony door. Through the glass he looked again on the construction site, still and crisp in the December cold, the sparse foundations sharing a sense of possibility with the pristine, manicured turf of a pitch before kick-off. Then he looked up at the sky. It still wasn't fully light, but the first strains of the day were coming through. It was something.

Like many men his age, the Old Man was in the habit of waking up early, putting on a smart outfit, and settling in his chair with nothing to do and the young day stretching, boundless, ahead of him. It wasn't clear how he had fallen into this trap; he certainly hadn't chosen, consciously, to adhere to this pattern. But his routine was much too brittle by now for him to change it. If it were up to him, for one thing, he would not spend so much time with the talking heads on the sports pages, those know-nothings who could barely string a sentence together. The latest gossip was all about the Argentinian. They said a well-known foreign side was ready to make an offer, and the club would have to accept. The only questions, supposedly, were around how much the club would get for him and how the finances of the deal might be structured.

The Old Man washed up his coffee cup and his saucer. He looked in the fridge and closed it again, averting his nose from the smell of a cheese past its best. Then he returned to his paper, starting now at the front. Local news shot through with local crimes: sex cases, vandalism, drink driving. Hospital waiting lists were longer than ever; a local councillor had defected from the idiots wearing blue to the idiots wearing red.

The Old Man thought he could feel the day outside pressing through the balcony doors, a sudden draught where the flat hadn't been finished to a proper standard. And this despite the heating having been on all morning. The Old Man's fingers were sticking to the thin newspaper, lifting off traces of print where he had been sweating. His wife liked it this way, but the artificial heat made him lethargic. He wanted to go for a walk to escape the stuffiness, but he didn't like to leave her when she was still in bed. And it would be cold, he knew, down by the river. The worst part was that winter was only just starting. He had seen his share of winters; he knew enough to recognise that this would be a bad one.

Nonetheless, he felt clammy, overdressed, in the forced heat. He had a desperate urge to turn down the thermostat, although he knew his wife would complain if it got too cold. He understood, of course; he too felt the cold in his joints. That very night, in fact, he would find himself cursing in bed because the discomfort in his fingers was keeping him awake. But that would come later.

For now, there was time before the football started – time to deal with, to kill. He looked over the top of the paper at the small Christmas tree in the corner of the room. He had bought it that week at the market, where he had gone shopping for her present. It was only a tiny thing, more weed than tree. Already, it had carpeted its pot with needles, and it looked silly with one miserly strand of tinsel draped over it, but his wife liked it all the same. The Old Man considered taking it down, but it seemed too soon for that. Instead, he got up and ate an apple.

He looked down at the site while he ate, but he didn't dare open the balcony doors, viewing the scene instead through the dusty glass. Again, there was nobody down there. A pair of gulls settled on the crane. The day grew lighter still.

The Old Man finished his apple and made to throw away what remained. Wrapping paper glinted from the bin by the kitchen sink. He dropped the core onto the paper, producing a harsh rustling, crumpling sound. At the same time, a noise came from his wife's bedroom, the sound of her stirring. The Old Man knew already that her chief concern during the game would be the Argentinian; he had long been her favourite player, and the Old Man expected to be asked about him again, even though he had told her already about him wanting to leave, forcing a move away from the club. And she wouldn't like the Irishman, the Old Man supposed, because she had never seen him play before. The Irishman was idiosyncratic in his style, and that was why the fans had been slow to warm to him. But he was good, the Irishman. He had something about him. And he was only young. The Old Man had learned that you had to make allowances for the young.

19

MOTHER TONGUE

THE ARGENTINIAN had been halfway gone for weeks, but now, at last, it was official.

Some of the fans had started saying on social media that he was overrated and had always had a bad attitude, but many of those same fans, just a few months ago, would have told you the Argentinian was the club's best-ever technical player, as good as any number ten in the league – barring, of course, the obvious exceptions. Now they would have to find a new number ten. There would be no chance for the fans to see off the Argentinian; he was already on the continent for his medical.

The year was closing out, and this game was the last before the transfer window opened on New Year's Day. A pre-contract agreement had already been settled, however, and the German conceded to the local press that the Argentinian was as good as sold. Part of it was that the Argentinian's family had never adjusted well to life in England. He had a young son and a new baby and a wife who, until now, had lived with him in a new-build in the countryside. It was very different to where they had lived before. The wife would stay until they sold the house, and then she would follow him to the continent as soon as the paperwork was signed.

The Young Man was sad to see the Argentinian go, but he was also glad that the transfer saga was over. It had been a distraction, and the other players didn't need it. Some of the fans still took it as an insult, but the Young Man was more sanguine about it now. He supposed there were bigger things to worry about. And the money from the Argentinian's sale would help strengthen the squad elsewhere. It was just one of those things, the reality of supporting a club of this stature.

It was a busy time for the Young Man, and the competing pressures on his attention stopped him from dwelling too much on the Argentinian's departure. He had plans for New Year's Eve, for one thing. He was going to a party with friends of his girlfriend. He had not met any of them before, and since his girlfriend had still not introduced him to her parents – or, indeed, to anyone in her life – he was interested to see what her friends were like. With the party in mind, he was in a good mood as he left his flat. It helped that he was off work for another week or so, a stretch in which he did not have to carry the absurd worries of the job he hated but could not escape, since he knew he would not find anything better. (He had his degree, of course, but so did everyone else.)

And it was good that Christmas was out of the way. It had been strange this year: his mother's first Christmas without parents, his first with a girlfriend. And it had come at the end of a difficult period, he reflected, considering his mounting worries, how he had pinned his happiness and his prospects on someone who never seemed more than one bad day from leaving, from becoming forever lost to him. Something that was chronic, he well knew, would never go away, never get better. Fold in those wider worries – the world's trajectory, the war, what sort of future might survive it – and it made the Old Man's advice seem like a cruel joke. When the Old Man closed his eyes, surely he did not also see keloid tracks running, like sleepers, across pale skin?

The Young Man stepped into the day, pushing these thoughts from his mind. He locked his front door and turned towards the bridge. Then it would be the familiar cut through, skirting the city centre, walking past the market, until he joined the throng of men and women heading for the ground. The stadium, the other side of the city, was just short of the new development, the plaza of chain restaurants and tower blocks by the river. It was a pleasant walk. The Young Man always enjoyed it. He usually put his headphones in and let his mind switch off as his legs carried him, today limping faintly but with no real pain. The walk was good for him, and besides, it was all he had.

The Young Man's consultant had told him to avoid high-impact exercise for the rest of his life. No running, no football; the Young Man remembered how, on the day of his diagnosis, he had felt suddenly hollow, as if an essential part of him had been scooped out with the onset of the illness. He would go on to feel the same about his work, his life, counting almost every day everything he was missing and wondering why these things had been taken from him. He thought he was cursed sometimes, wondered if he had been bad in an earlier life. But when he had told his girlfriend about his condition, she had merely shrugged in response.

Okay, she had said.

They had been playing mobile chess at the time, sitting on his bed with her phone between them, on the covers. It had been his idea to play, but she was winning. She barely looked up from her queen, which was under threat from his encroaching pawn. He watched her finger hover over the screen, a devastated nail lingering above the symbol of a pointed crown. (The queen was the most precious offensive piece in the game, worth almost twice as much as a rook and able to move an unlimited number of squares in any direction.)

Okay? he asked.

She smiled. I just mean there are worse things that could be wrong with you, she said. These things happen, right? It's just life. So it goes, and all that.

She had laughed, then, and he had been able to believe, for a moment, that perhaps in his past life he had been okay, after all.

The Young Man tried to hold on to this notion as he walked, the river dark and swollen beneath the bridge. It seemed like there ought to be more than one river, the way it weaved and kinked, but it was the same river which knotted itself about the heart of the city, down by his flat, and then went off towards the stadium and the new development. Beyond to places he had heard about but never seen.

As the Young Man turned to cross the bridge, he anticipated the presence of the beggar. He was used, by now, to being stopped and asked for change. In recent months the beggar had grown a wild beard. The last time the Young Man had seen him, he had been slumped forward on his mat of cardboard, sleeping through the early afternoon. A coat worn over a coat with both hoods up. Today, however, there was no sign of him. It wasn't clear where else he might have gone, but the Young Man supposed it was too cold to be homeless now. It was like everything he tried not to read about in the news; there was nothing he could do to help anyone other than her, who was reluctant to let him, and so he preferred not to think about it – about any of it. He could not even help himself, not in any of the ways that really mattered. Only she could do that; only another person's love held so much restorative power.

·

The Old Man was also making ready for the final game of the calendar year. In fact, he was already at the turnstile, waving his ticket at the barcode scanner but holding it upside down, back to front, so that the young ticket attendant had to take the stub and show the Old Man, not for the first time, how to position it against the reader. A queue had formed behind him. Then there was a click and a green light, and the Old Man passed through the turnstile. He felt vindicated, for a moment, in his refusal to use one of the cheap plastic cards they were always trying to foist on him, insisting on real, physical tickets instead. He had seen no beggars on his walk to the ground, but he never saw beggars in summer, either, so why should he have seen one today?

·

Across town, the Young Man, as he was walking, was thinking about how strange it was that the calendar year was nearly up and yet the football year was only half finished. There were times when it was not helpful to think of a year as finishing in December, because now they were not really at the end of the year but in its crucial midpoint, when the fixtures came every few days. Weeknight football, distinct atmospheres at those matches played after early sunsets, under the lights. Likewise, it didn't help to think of there being four seasons in a year when the calendar year was actually comprised, in a meaningful sense, of two half-seasons.

As the Young Man was thinking this, a gust of chill wind came from behind one of the grand town-centre buildings, an old brewery converted into flats. It occurred to him that this country was an uncommonly cold and mean place, and there was a part of him that wanted to be elsewhere, although he knew he would never really leave. It was much easier to talk about leaving, as some of his old friends from university did, than to actually leave. He knew nobody who had. And he had ties here: the club, his girlfriend. He would not find replicated anywhere else the exact feel of English football matches, the unique blend of humour and rage and despondency and joy and the pretence at violence, an ironic, ritualised throwback rather than an actual desire to hurt anyone. Nobody else got it like they did. And then he thought of the Old Man, who would surely understand what he meant. He felt for the Old Man on days like today, because he knew he struggled with the cold.

And of course, these thoughts and worries were not unique to the Young Man. Here was one of very few things he was able to share with one of his heroes, usually so remote from the fans and their everyday concerns. Because while the Argentinian really hadn't minded so much (in fact, he had enjoyed the money and made a good job of spending it, for a young man who was sober and clean and married), life in England had never agreed with his wife. The coldness and the customs seemed too alien to ever acclimatise to. The wind was relentless, depressing. Taxes were going up again to pay for the fallout of the plague years, the distant war, and they had started to think about schools: where they would send their eldest, what language he would grow up speaking, what ought to be his cultural default. At home, they spoke Spanish to the baby. And on the continent, in their new home in an old country, they would do the same.

20

#VAMOS!

THE YOUNG MAN WAS hungover from the party, and he was on a comedown. It was New Year's Day, they were playing away from home, and he had stayed over at his girlfriend's house. This combination of factors meant he was glad, for once, that he did not have a ticket for today's game. He didn't miss many games, but when he did, it was always with good reason. He could watch today's match online. His girlfriend would join him, most likely.

The Young Man assumed the previous night had been a success. They had arrived fashionably late at a city-centre flat rented by a friend of his girlfriend. The Young Man, carrying a plastic bag heavy with cans of lager and premixed cocktails, kissed his girlfriend on the step while they were waiting to be buzzed in. He told her she looked beautiful, and she smiled her thanks. Her friends were excited to see them together.

They said they had heard a lot about him, and he was greeted by a procession of young women offering tipsy smiles and hugs, good-natured jokes. The smells of competing perfumes lingered on his cheek.

The flat turned out to be an impossibly neat space, gently lit and softly furnished in the way that only women's apartments can be. They played a succession of drinking games, the music seeming to grow louder with every drained can, the bottom of each glass. The Young Man laughing and dancing with her friends, talking about football with the other boyfriends as one of them rolled a twenty in the bathroom, shouting through the closed door about the January transfer window. The others all followed Big Six sides, but they were alright, and the Young Man thought his girlfriend's friends were good fun. At midnight they had counted down and watched fireworks through the window, on the TV. The Young Man kissed his girlfriend and wished her a Happy New Year before accepting a peck on the cheek from the friend whose apartment it was. All night his girlfriend had been quiet and watchful, but the Young Man had come to learn that she could be like that sometimes, and there was nothing he could do to help her snap out of it. They had slipped away to her house-share in the early hours, he having forgotten all his worries and she having amassed more of her own.

The Young Man had gone to bed with a ringing in his ears and a pain behind his eyes and having enjoyed himself greatly. He thought he had made a good impression on his girlfriend's friends. But then his girlfriend woke complaining of a headache, shifting away when he reached out for her in bed.

Did you enjoy yourself? he asked, rubbing sleep from his eyes as he waited for the room to take shape around him.

What?

Last night, he said. Did you have fun?

I don't want to talk about last night, she said.

What? There was a pause while he sat up in bed, adjusting the pillows. Then, Why not?

I just don't, okay?

The Young Man laughed. I don't understand.

Please, just drop it.

The Young Man was left wondering at her dissatisfaction as he went downstairs to make toast and coffee, grateful there was no sign of her housemates in the kitchen they all shared. He checked social media as the kettle boiled. The Argentinian's transfer had been officially announced. A social media manager had composed a message to the fans of his new club, saying how excited he was to get started. To fans of his old club, like the Young Man, the Argentinian had posted a message of thanks. It was obvious that the Argentinian hadn't written it himself because the message was in perfect English and used a series of emojis which seemed out of keeping with his character. But the words were touching and strangely profound, from the Young Man's perspective, although he would have struggled to articulate exactly why he was so moved by a message so obviously insincere. He supposed he was feeling fragile after the night before, was what it was.

The Young Man returned to his girlfriend's room. She thanked him for the coffee, the toast. He got back into her bed and drank his coffee and ate his toast while he looked at his phone, reading messages of thanks and abuse from fellow fans, all in response to the Argentinian's announcement. His girlfriend was silent, looking out the window as she ate. He could feel, above him, the weight of the ceiling. In many ways, it felt like a bad day to be awake, but at least he had the football to look forward to. He asked her if she would watch it with him, but her response was noncommittal. He asked if she wanted him to go back to his place and leave her alone, but her response, again, gave no indication of what she really wanted. He was in no hurry to get out of bed, so he stayed where he was.

The Young Man requisitioned her laptop to watch the match. At the last home game, the Old Man had told him to keep an eye on the young Englishman at right-back, to see how good the Englishman was at reading the game. Today the Young Man made a point of watching him.

Even as the saga with the wantaway Argentinian approached its apogee, the young Englishman had been quietly going about his business, seemingly unaffected by all the speculation, the disruption. As with the Argentinian, there had been paper talk about bigger and much wealthier clubs wanting his signature, but the Englishman never commented on these rumours. Nor had he allowed them to affect his performance or his focus.

The Englishman was what you would call a consummate professional – a trait unusual in a boy of nineteen. But then, there were many things about the young Englishman which were unusual in a boy of nineteen. Like the car he drove and the house he lived in. And the fiancée – a girl he had known from school – who was expecting, but she hadn't told anyone yet. And his sobriety, and his refusal to smoke or do drugs, and the way he had stopped going to lessons when he was still very young, so that he didn't really understand the most basic principles of mathematics and didn't always conjugate his verbs properly when messaging friends and teammates or speaking with reporters before and after the games. Unusual, also, was the contract with his agent, and the sponsorship deal with a major sportswear manufacturer. Perhaps the oddest thing, for a boy of his age, was that he, like the Argentinian, paid someone else to use social media for him.

And yet, in other ways, the Englishman was like many other nineteen-year-old boys. He didn't like to do his own laundry, cooking, or shopping, and other people generally took care of these things for him. But he was insulated from the world in ways the Young Man could only dream of, and though they were both young men who wore the same shirt on matchdays, there was more that divided them than united them. The Young Man was only ever pretending, for one, when he wore his replica kit; he was six years older than the young Englishman, but he was the one who was playing dress-up, a childish game.

And the Englishman would always have his wealth to draw on; he was well rewarded for the sacrifices he made. Some of the fans thought he might be called up to the national team soon, but others, like the Young Man, thought he still needed time to grow into his game. Either way, he was a credit to the club, and at the same time as envying the neat certainty of his life – training on weekdays, match on Saturday, rest day, repeat – the Young Man was strangely proud of the Englishman. He felt an almost brotherly connection to him, although he would never admit something so embarrassing. Not least because having a younger brother seemed the next best thing to having a family of his own – that impossible wish he so rarely spoke aloud.

As the Young Man watched the Englishman, starring in the stolen livestream on his girlfriend's laptop, he felt for a moment as if he was outside of himself taking in this scene, replete with his girlfriend beside him, in the third person. He asked her then if she was okay, and she said she was fine. It was not a vintage game, and he was glad not to have travelled for it.

The commentary which came from the laptop's tiny speakers was foreign, indecipherable, and the pitch looked wrong – off, somehow – in the low resolution of the stream. The Young Man tried to focus on the touchline. He watched the vertex where the corner flag was; he fixed his stare for one whole minute, then another. In time, the markings lost all their significance, like a word repeated too many times aloud, so that he could only process as a shape and not as a symbol the obscure white of the touchline, hazy against the green. Then came the Englishman, sliding against an opposition forward and dispossessing him into the hoarding. The Young Man smiled and thought of the Old Man. His girlfriend stirred beside him. She rose and left the room. The Young Man waited until half-time, and then he went to check on her, imagining as he descended the stairs what he would say to the young Englishman were he in that dressing room with him, were he able to thank him for his service to the club and all that it meant to the fans, to men like him.

21

FINE WITHOUT YOU

The Old Man was in hospital, and all his wife had to say about it was that she didn't know why he had spent all that money on a season ticket if he was going to miss half the games. He was admitted on the Friday afternoon, and they said they wanted to keep him in for observations overnight. Kick-off was at midday on Saturday. There was no way he would make it.

The Old Man looked up at his wife – a stare of sad exasperation, some final tether of restraint finally snapping – and said he hadn't planned on being in hospital this weekend, had he? If it was up to him, he would much rather be at the bloody game. He did not say it aloud, but neither had he planned on being apart from his wife for more than a few hours.

The Old Man was not as worried about himself as he was about leaving his wife on her own overnight. But the doctor, clearly one of the better ones, gently refuted his suggestion that he was being needlessly fussed over. And so his wife stayed with him until she grew tired, and then she took a taxi back to the flat. Of course, they had no children they could call on to help them, and they didn't know their neighbours. They weren't even certain if anyone else lived on their floor. Of all the faces the Old Man knew, almost all of them were acquaintances from the football. His wife had her friends, but since selling their house and moving to the other side of the city, she had seen much less of them. They wouldn't be much good in a situation like this, anyway. For the Old Man there had been no choice but to call the taxi company and make sure his wife knew to phone him if there was a problem.

She had laughed when he said that. She said, You're the sick one, in the hospital, and you're worrying about me. It ought to be the other way round.

I'm not sick, he said. I'm fine.

Why are you in the hospital then, if you're fine?

The Old Man shook his head. Can't believe I've got to miss another bloody game, he said.

That was when the doctor came back. There were just a few more tests, she said. They would know a lot more about what had happened once they had the results. The Old Man feared a restless night, rattling coughs and moans down the hall, but in the event, he slept surprisingly well, drifting into a velvet blackness and waking to another matchday in which he would play no part.

Later that morning – having been sufficiently prodded and scanned and questioned about his health history, the long-ago deaths of his parents, his medications – the Old Man finally found himself in the process of being discharged. His wife was there with him. She had spent the night alone in the flat and seemed not to have minded. But the Old Man had awful visions. Although these days she very rarely cooked, he imagined her having left the hob on, pans melting and smoking foully atop the stove. In his head he saw all the taps running, the bath overflowing. He feared he would unlock the door and find the whole building burning or flooded or both. His wife, however, insisted that she had been fine. She said he worried too much. The Old Man feared he would see about that, soon enough.

•

For the Young Man – who had all this ahead of him, all this to look forward to – it was just another matchday. The first suggestion that something might be wrong was when he emerged from the concourse and saw the seat beside his was vacant, long after the time when the Old Man liked to get there. The team sheets had already been announced, and now they were piping that same pop music into the stands, the playlist unchanged week on week. The notes and the voices lost their definition when they were contorted through the speakers like that, louder than anyone needed. It seemed to flatten the music. On the pitch below, the players were out for their warm-ups.

Surprised and strangely disquieted by the Old Man's absence, the Young Man returned to the concourse for a pint, although he struggled to enjoy it. He came back out as the ground was filling up. There was still no sign of the Old Man. Even when kick-off came, the seat beside his remained empty. It might have been the only empty seat on the terrace. Out in the centre circle, the Finn won the toss, and he chose to defend the goal in front of the terrace in the first half. They would attack it in the second.

By now, the Old Man was a firm fixture in the Young Man's mind, as permanent and as much a part of the stadium as any of the stands or the corner flags or the dugout from which the German and his staff and the substitutes watched the game. It didn't feel right without the Old Man there. And this, the first home game of the year, was a match of significance. The Young Man feared his neighbour's absence might even be a bad omen.

But these worries lasted all of five minutes before, in a moment of brilliance, the young Englishman sold a dummy to their left winger and tore past him. Seconds later, he pulled a variation of the same skill to elude their left-back, leaving him on the turf with his legs knotted together. Applause rained down from the stands, shouts of encouragement, as the Englishman carried the ball away from the Young Man, heading for the opposite end of the pitch, the other goal. This was what the fans wanted from their team; this progressive, attacking instinct was why the German had been made manager in the first place.

The flank seemed to open before the Englishman, endless white paint stretching out as far as anyone could see – out beyond the fans in the opposite terrace and out across the river and beyond the city, even, across the sea and all the way east, to the mined and cratered farmland on the edge of the continent. A line across which every home fan in that stadium could be arranged, a line unifying the loci of those disparate lives. A line distinct from the scars that still rose in the Young Man's mind, the powder of the previous week's party.

The Englishman, alone in those acres of space, drove to the byline, watching as yellow jerseys flooded the box. A centre-half peeled off to close him down, but the Englishman had already gone too far to be stopped. Now he weighed the ball, calculating cost and benefit, risk and reward. A second passed before, at last, he whipped in his cross. The Finn, not usually known for his aerial ability, was unmarked, and he met the ball with his head, cushioning it perfectly for the Irishman – a lay-off straight from the training ground. All the home fans stood at once, watching as the ball bounced, as the Irishman contorted his body, making ready to hit it. Then came the laces of the Irishman, the connection everyone had been waiting for, and the fans all opened their mouths and raised their arms as the ball was blasted beyond the keeper and into the corner of the net. The home fans made that universal, inexplicable noise that signifies the scoring of a goal – part shout, part cheer, pure joy – and then the goal music came on. Some of the supporters gripped each other's hands; many waved scarves above their heads. The Irishman, small in the distance and strangely vivid, like a freshly painted figurine, ran over to the corner flag to celebrate. The away end went quiet, and the Young Man joined the men around him in turning to the block of travelling fans, their angry gestures bouncing harmlessly off the jubilant home faithful, armoured as they were by their joy. One-nil on your big day out, came the chant.

•

On a new and still unfinished residential development not far from the stadium, the Old Man used an electronic fob to open the door to his building. His wife followed behind. At that moment, a roar – a sound like waves breaking – rose in the near distance. The Old Man knew what it meant; there had been a goal, and he smiled to himself at the thought. He and his wife made for the lifts. He supposed he might even make it to the stadium in time for the second half, if he got a move on.

A minute or so later, the Old Man was leading his wife down the carpeted communal hallway to their apartment. There was silence inside the building, broken only by the sound of their steps, his heavy breathing. Paint smells, as ever. His wife followed wordlessly behind. She seemed, in the Old Man's mind, to be acting like a guilty child waiting to be discovered, and the jubilation of the goal had already been swallowed by a mounting dread, the sick suspicion that devastation was waiting beyond the door. He stopped at the welcome mat, sorting through his various keys for the one which would let them into the apartment. He slid the key into the lock and turned it. He depressed the door handle and pushed. The door swung open, and he stepped quickly inside, casting his gaze across the unsegmented space which served as a kitchen, living room and dining room.

There was no visible evidence of flooding, no smoke or fire damage. One plate, one cup and one fork were drying on the rack. The tea towel had been folded neatly and draped over the oven door handle. The only thing amiss was the ceiling light, which had been left on even though the day was streaming through the uncurtained balcony door. The Old Man snapped the light switch and turned, bewildered, to his wife, who was smiling at him from the doorway.

You see, she said. I was fine without you.

22

IN HIS TIME

THE REFEREE, SURELY SAVOURING the attention of so many, hesitated for just long enough to let doubt calcify in the hivemind of the fans. Then he pointed to the spot. It was a penalty for the opposition, as the Young Man had known it would be. He had seen it coming – the referee looking to the linesman, the waving flag, the shrill whistle – even before the Norwegian went lunging in at the edge of the box, a clumsy challenge to mark his surprise return to the first team.

Cheers came now from the home mob, accented with particularly loud jeers from the block of hardcore fans beside the away supporters. The Young Man looked over at that hateful, triumphant crowd, trying to sift from the great, mindless mass the faces of individual beings. He was looking for humanity, but all he saw were finger signs and ironic waves, his fellow fans surrounded and outshouted by the febrile home support. It was one of those games where the referee's decisions kept going against them, and the Young Man thought of it as a karmic rebalancing from that spell, a short while back, when they had seemed to get the benefit of every doubt. No more.

It took just a few seconds for the decision to be checked and confirmed; the penalty stood. The Young Man, like everyone else in the away section, shouted, waved his scarf, did everything he could to put off the opposition captain, who had positioned the ball on the spot in preparation for the penalty. The Dutchman, in the goal beneath them, was up to his usual antics: making himself big, trying to get the penalty taker's attention, delaying the kick while he fetched his water bottle and then set it back down behind the goal having not taken so much as a sip. The referee allowed the Dutchman a few more seconds to adjust his gloves before, under pressure from the opposition, he booked him for time wasting. This only stoked the antagonistic joy of the home fans, and now the stadium – a legacy of the Olympic Games, a decade on – began to bubble and fizz like a cauldron. It was a round stadium, with a running track between the fans and the pitch. The Young Man hated the place: it was all new, all artifice. After the penalty had gone in – the scorer celebrating in the Dutchman's face and the home fans breaking into the opening strains of their famous anthem – he hated it even more.

The laughs of the home fans: individuals subsumed into a goading, graceless mass. The Young Man loved it when his team was winning, but it was awful to be on the other end of it. And today it felt like a personal insult, after the week he had endured: argument after argument with his girlfriend, who had not wanted him to go today but whom he had defied to be here. Who still would not introduce him to her parents, which only made him think there was something wrong with him or, worse, that part of her was still not committed to their relationship. Who had laughed when he said – earnest and voluble after too many midweek pints, post-work drinks – that the best and hardest thing anyone could be was a parent. But she was not well, he had to remind himself sometimes. She deserved allowances too.

The Young Man would not, however, make allowances for the home fans as they sang throughout the half, as they jeered and waved. After the restart, time for a couple more beers to be downed, the atmosphere inside the stadium grew tense, and the occasion developed an edge. The usual chants were repurposed, and the air above the stands was flecked with threats. The Young Man had to remind himself that it was mostly in jest, although this was one of those fixtures where there could be some unpleasantness. The home supporters were known as a tough lot; their hardcore fans (ultras, they called themselves, an embarrassing pretence) worked tirelessly to uphold their bad reputation. Derbies were known to be particularly bloody, and when rivals from the capital came here to play, the police massed like an army. On those days, they handed down stadium bans like confetti, but still the numbers swelled, still they sang and fought. Football had changed, but sometimes it seemed that nobody had bothered to let the fans know.

A few years ago – after this new stadium had been leased from the government and refitted and painted in the colours of the club – the supporters were uprooted from their old home and transplanted, without consultation, into this regenerated tract of the capital. They were closer, now, to the city proper, further from their roots. Still, the home fans were trying to make the best of it; many of them were solid, working people like those the Young Man had grown up with, like those who also populated the town where his girlfriend had been born.

Most of them came to the games just to let off steam. That was fair enough, the Young Man supposed; he could appreciate those impulses. The problem was what happened afterwards, after the game. After the Young Man had trudged down the steps and out of the stadium with one final glance back at the scoreboard, the numbers taunting him, the dash between them cruel and evocative. After his phone signal came back and he saw he had missed a call and a series of messages from his girlfriend, none of them good.

Today was no derby, but there was still a strong police presence around the ground. Here the officers went to especially great lengths to ensure the home and away fans didn't mix before or after the games. They shepherded the travelling fans out through distinct gates and funnelled them towards the station, practically with their own escort of officers. Some of the officers rode horses. In the eyes of the nearest horse, the Young Man looked for a reflection of himself but saw only emotions unknowable to him. Then he was being nudged forward by the bodies behind, overcome by a sense of déjà vu, and he had to look away.

The trouble started when a core of marauding home fans pushed through the escort, the police much too slow to contain them. There were marked and unmarked vans parked everywhere, but it seemed nobody was in them. Everyone was shouting, and the Young Man felt a shove behind him, a sharp pressure in the small of his back which almost sent him sprawling to the ground. The police stepped in now, in twos and threes, but they only made things worse. Replica jerseys clashed horribly with one another and with the police uniforms, creating a sickening, psychedelic effect.

There was some swinging, but few of the men were sober or motivated enough to make a serious go of it. The Young Man covered his head and moved forward, lost in a shifting tide of bodies and deafened, for the moment, by shouts. He stumbled past a man kneeling by the roadside, holding his nose. Blood ran like ketchup down the front of the man's yellow shirt. The Young Man thought about stopping to ask if he was okay, but by now he just wanted to get home. He was not interested in violence; he never had been. He didn't consider boxing or martial arts to be real sports any more than motor racing or pool or dressage. He only went to the football because he enjoyed the atmosphere; he liked to be among so many people who were, for a couple of hours a week, completely aligned in purpose and spirit. It was good to share these dreams – abstract as they were – with a crowd. Such ugliness had, for him, never been part of the bargain.

Even after the home fans had been largely driven off, the worst and slowest of the troublemakers detained by the roadside, the atmosphere stayed sour. The Young Man supposed this was how football used to be, in the decades before his sport was commercialised, sanitised. He would have to ask the Old Man at the next home game. He knew the Old Man had travelled all over with the team when he was younger, and it was likely that he had seen much worse in his time. Back then, more than a few nutters only went to the football to cause trouble: fighting for control of the terraces, hunting opposition colours on estate streets after the game. They did not care for beauty, and their legacy tainted the reputation of football fans even now.

The Young Man, for his part, recognised that there was a balance to be struck. He didn't agree with the efforts of many football clubs to attract more families to the games, dampening the occasion into a whimsical and child-friendly day out (although in his own pixellated visions of the future, he imagined inducting a son to the team, teaching him the songs). He liked to be among people who took it seriously; he liked those fans who were loud and committed. But that didn't mean anyone had to get hurt.

A policeman ran past, the radio at his hip chattering away into the clotted air. The away fans were being kettled, almost, although they weren't the ones who had started the trouble, and now the ranks of police on either side pressed them closer together. The Young Man could hear the panting of horses even over the chant which started up among the knot of away fans. The Young Man joined in, but the singing fizzled out very quickly. He looked in the direction of the station. It was close. Behind the station there were tower blocks, and behind them, not much further, the skyscrapers of the financial district loomed spectral, offices and apartment buildings rising like teeth or else spines aback some great beast. This vista, smeared with the hi-vis shades of football kits and police uniforms and scored by the sounds of ebbing violence off to the side, presented itself as a nightmare mirage to the Young Man. He wondered if the beer had been bad. He was very eager to get to the station now.

In the distance, a siren blared once. Someone gripped

the Young Man by the arm. Beside him, a horse's flank was steaming. The Old Man would want to hear about this skirmish in another city, in the shadow of another stadium. And once he had taken it in, he would no doubt offer his own judgement about how it had always been this way and how the true spirit of the game was something that couldn't be repressed forever beneath the slogans of corporate sponsors, the logos of finance partners, and the polite chatter of hospitality boxes. How much had changed in his lifetime and how much of it was for the worse.

The Young Man almost smiled imagining the Old Man's tone, a measure of comfort as he approached the station. Almost. But for now, the Young Man just wanted to press on, to get home, to put the game and the dropped points and the eye of the horse – glossy and weighty as a billiard ball – as far into his past as these things would go.

23

TEAM SHEETS

THE OLD MAN STOOD at the sink with an envelope in his hand. He was dressed for football: thick black coat; black trousers; running shoes in which he had never once ran; and his lucky scarf, loose around his shoulders. He should have been at the ground by now, and yet the Old Man could not bring himself to leave the apartment.

He was acutely conscious of the envelope. He weighed it in his mind, felt the residue of the glue clinging to his fingertips. It had already been opened, the letter inside unfolded and read and re-folded and returned to the envelope. The name was right; there had been no mistake. The address was here, this apartment. The place he could not stop thinking of as their new home, even though they had been here for over a year already. The Old Man still had half a mind to give his old address, whenever he was asked. He kept tripping over the new postcode, needed a mnemonic to remember it. New or old, his wife did not think of this place as home at all.

The team sheets would be out soon, and still the Old Man did not move, did not set off for the ground. There was talk in the papers that the Finn had injured himself again in training. They said the manager would have to keep the Norwegian in the eleven and go with just the young Irishman up front. It was a risk to deploy the Irishman on his own, to rely on the Norwegian in midfield, but the German had no choice.

The Old Man shivered, despite his many layers. It was raining, as it had been all day, and he knew he would get wet on the walk. When he strained to listen, as he did now, he could hear the rain against the decking of the balcony. Whenever the wind picked up, great lashings of water came slantwise against the balcony door. All morning his wife had been passing comment on the weather, asking if it was wise for him to go out in it. She didn't say he would catch his death, but that was clearly what she was thinking. It didn't help that the Old Man was feeling particularly fragile today. He had been woken up early by his joints that morning. The cold did that now.

The Old Man, as if doubting his own memory, withdrew the letter from the envelope. He set the envelope on the counter. Then he unfolded the letter and read it, again. His wife was in her chair. She wasn't looking at him; she didn't seem to care or even notice, in fact, that he had not moved from his place, standing before the sink. He looked like he was about to do the washing up, but there were no dishes on the side.

When he had finished re-reading the letter, the Old Man looked up and shook his head. He considered, for a moment, putting the letter in the sink and opening the taps. Instead he opened the cabinet beside the sink, in which the bin was hidden. He dropped in the envelope but kept hold of the letter. Then, without saying anything, he walked over to the balcony door. He unclasped the lock and slid the door open. It was heavy, and it took all his strength to get it moving.

The rain came that much louder with the door open, but even over the deluge, the Old Man could hear a plane, a fast jet, tearing somewhere above the clouds. There had been helicopters earlier; their frequency seemed to be increasing again. But his attention was not on the activity at the air bases or the faraway escalations of the war. He did not have the luxury of caring about things which were not immediately pertinent to him. And since he did not have children or grandchildren, he was not as invested in the future as he might have been. As younger men were.

The Old Man stepped onto the balcony. Out here, the air itself seemed soaked through. He breathed in and out, tasting rain, and then he held the letter over the railing and, recognising the strangeness of his own impulses, let it fall. It pirouetted in clean air, suspended for a fraction of a second, and then the rain caught it, the paper yielding to the weight of the water, pushed down and out of sight. The Old Man didn't see it land. He had already stepped back into the living room; he was already shutting the balcony door. His wife looked up now for the first time.

Are you okay, she said.

I'm fine, said the Old Man. I have to get going now.

Okay, she said. She smiled sweetly, and the Old Man recognised her smile as a lost expression from her youth. A smile almost entirely buried beneath the weight of time, emerging these days only fleetingly, a flash of who she had once been. I hope they win, she added.

That smile. The Old Man was stunned for a moment – stunned and crushed – but he concealed his discomfort before she had a chance to catch on. He forced a smile in return.

Let's hope so, he said.

When he was at the front door, he turned back and said, Call me if you need anything.

I'll be fine, she said. Don't forget your brolly.

He picked up his umbrella from its place by the door and waved it at her to show he had remembered.

•

But nothing could really protect against wind and rain like this, the kind that blows sidewards and comes at you with the force of buckshot. The Young Man knew this, for in that moment he was wrestling with his own umbrella, head bowed as he made his way down the road leading to the stadium. He was soon forced to give up, collapsing the umbrella before the wind wrenched it from his grip or broke it. All around him, men and women in billowing raincoats and glistening ponchos were fighting against the sudden gust: some laughing, some shouting their misplaced anger at the weather systems responsible for their difficulties. Everywhere it smelled of rain: rain on grass, rain on concrete, rain on skin.

The Young Man came from the direction opposite the terrace, and so he had to walk around the ground to get to their designated entrance. Today, fans were milling about like refugees beneath the eaves of the club shop, bodies pressed together in the precious dry. Many wore jackets with moisture beading on the hoods and the shoulders and the sleeves. A few of the hardier sorts were still lining up, despite the weather, for burgers and hotdogs from the vans. The Young Man moved past these queues, heading for the terrace. He was soaked by the time he got to cover, darting the final metres through the doorway to the turnstile. He touched his card to the reader. He waited for the beep and the green light, and then he pushed through the gate with a nod of thanks for the man behind the glass.

More people than usual were standing around in the concourse – driven inside by the weather, no doubt. Most were wearing black, but the crowd was touched with yellow nonetheless: the hems of shirts hanging down beneath jackets, flashes of club scarves poking through at the collar. A few men were walking around in their jerseys, the sodden fabric plastered, translucent, to their bodies. Days like today made the Young Man grateful that the terrace was covered.

He knew today's game would be tough, although he dared to hope the conditions might help. He looked at his phone, but he was a few minutes early for the team sheets. Nor was there any update on social media about the Finn. He did have a message from his girlfriend, however: a link to an article about what they were calling the Great Resignation, a loose movement of the dissatisfied young (people like themselves), who had turned their backs on demeaning and unfulfilling work after the plague years. The Young Man saw the headline, but he wanted to read the article before replying. He bought a beer and read as he drank. It was dangerous, this kind of wishful thinking. He had been struck before by sudden, awful glimpses of the futility of his work, that set of tasks which occupied most of his waking hours and demanded almost all his emotional and mental bandwidth. But anyone could convince themselves easily enough that they were wasting their life. Most people were, the Young Man supposed, but the trick was to fill your free time with distractions, like the football, before the truth of it overwhelmed you.

The Young Man had meant to compose a reply along these lines in his seat (thanking her also for thinking of him, grateful as ever for scraps of her attention, proof of another human being's love). But when the Young Man eventually emerged into the cold of the terrace he noted, again, that the Old Man wasn't there.

Instead of writing back to his girlfriend, the Young Man sat and listened to the drumming of rain against the corrugated metal roof as he considered and then discarded various explanations for the Old Man's absence. Illness, death, sudden loss of interest? There were no good reasons why he might miss two consecutive home games, although the Young Man recognised it was still early, and so he held on to the hope that the Old Man might yet make it in time for kick-off. He was desperate to tell the Old Man about the previous week, the motes of violence which swam, still, among his memories of their last game. And the weather, and the rumours about the Finn, the day's probable line-up. He supposed the Old Man would have plenty to say about all that. But for now, there was no Old Man to talk to. There was only his unoccupied seat, the moulded plastic flaring bright yellow, the colour of a warning flag.

The Young Man was jolted from his thoughts by a distant

strain of thunder. The thunderclap intensified, and then it grew louder, closer, until the jet passed overhead and moved on, beyond the Young Man's frame of reference. Of course, he too had heard the jets and the helicopters earlier that day, a frenzy of activity at the air bases. The experts on the news were saying that prices everywhere would go up because of the war. People on social media were saying nobody was safe, that the war might expand in scope and intensity. History had started up again, they said. But the Young Man didn't like to think about it too much, and he supposed that if the football was going ahead as normal then everything was probably fine for now. Annihilation could wait for ninety minutes.

The team sheets were soon announced, and it was as the supporters had all feared: no Finn, the Irishman alone up front, the Norwegian behind him. The Young Man shook his head, assembling the formation in his mind as the announcer read the names and numbers. It was all wrong; the Norwegian didn't fit. The Young Man rose to his feet, wincing at a stab of pain, and returned to the concourse.

He was immediately overwhelmed by the warmth and the closeness of the air, heavy with the competing smells of beer and damp human bodies. The Young Man picked a path through the faintly steaming crowd and joined the queue at the bar. He thought about the Old Man, wondering again at possible reasons for his absence. And then the obvious explanation struck him; the weather had probably deterred him from arriving so early. He would almost certainly show up in his own time, probably any minute now. He might even be in his seat already, wondering at the whereabouts of the Young Man.

And so it transpired. The Young Man emerged from the

concourse and smiled at the sight of the Old Man. He was there; he had taken up his position while the Young Man had been inside, composing a suitable reply to his girlfriend and drinking to guard against the cold.

Hello, said the Young Man, easing past his neighbour.

Hello, said the Old Man.

What time do you call this?

The Old Man looked up at the corrugated roof of the terrace, gesturing at the sky. Bloody rain kept me from leaving. I thought I'd wait for it to clear, but no luck. So now I'm late, and I got rained on anyway.

The Young Man laughed. How have you been?

Oh, you know, the Old Man said. You?

I'm alright, thanks, yeah. Not sure about this line-up though.

Me neither. But it's not like he's got much choice, is it?

Exactly.

They fell into silence, watching the rain fall on the pitch. The stadium announcer was standing near the centre circle, an assistant with a clipboard holding a massive umbrella over them both. The set-piece coach and a member of the rival backroom staff were talking at the mouth of the tunnel. They clasped hands and embraced before returning to their respective dugouts. A small pack of children, all of them holding miniature flags and sheathed in disposable ponchos, was being led around the length of the pitch by a man in a club-branded raincoat. There was never any shortage of small intrigue and diversionary spectacle in the minutes before kick-off. Both men were glad to be at the stadium, despite the wet and the cold; there was no awkwardness in them sitting quietly and watching these things, taking them in.

When the silence was eventually broken, it was the Old Man who spoke.

Listen, he said. I was thinking. Let me take your phone number in case I can't make it to another game. You can take my ticket and bring your missus or whoever in my place. You know, just in case I have to miss any more this season.

Thank you, said the Young Man. That's kind of you. I'll do the same, of course.

The Old Man scoffed. He held out his phone: a downmarket but functional model, a few iterations out of date. Here, he said. You can put your number in. Not like I've got people lining up to come with me, but thanks all the same.

The Young Man smiled and took the phone. He opened the contacts app and made to add a new entry to the short roll-call of the Old Man's connections. He recognised the names of a couple of taxi firms and one of the restaurants in the city centre. The number for the club's ticket office had been saved as well. A couple of doctors. A woman's name.

There you go, said the Young Man. Text me, and I'll save your number.

Will do. The Old Man pocketed his phone. The Young Man was strangely touched. He felt a distant melancholy, something he could not quite place, but stirred into that feeling was a happiness at the Old Man's reasoning, at the offer which had already brought them closer and which seemed so much like a pretext.

24

ASCENSION

In the space of a few months, the young Irishman had been propelled from the obscurity of the academy to the breathless altitudes of the first team. He had been the obvious man of the match last time out, deputising for the injured Finn, and already he was establishing a growing reputation. They said in the papers and on social media that he was one to watch. He was only twenty years old, but now all the broadcasters wanted to interview him after the games. In the dressing room, his fellow professionals had started talking to him like he was a man. In the boardroom, they were making noises about a new contract. Among his friends from the academy, very little was said to his face, but a great deal of praise was posted on social media. It was a lot to take in.

The Young Man had, of course, witnessed the Irishman's rapid ascension from his own vantage point in the stands. And he had been as surprised as anyone that of all their players it should be this man – with his slow eyes and that indescribable, laboured style of locomotion – who should demonstrate such an instinctive sense for the game.

The Young Man and the Old Man had celebrated together last week when the Irishman scored the third goal, completing his first senior hat-trick. It felt like something unreal, something imagined. Even now, the Young Man could not say with certainty whether the Old Man had really grabbed him by the shoulders when the ball hit the net. The Old Man shaking him slightly, flashing his discoloured teeth and laughing almost manically at the Irishman's brilliance. Eyes as wide as they went, a look that seemed to knock years off him. And there was pride, too, there among the other things. For whom, the Young Man could not say with certainty. He hoped to see more of the Irishman today.

He had spent the night at his girlfriend's house. When his phone went off with an alarm, she rolled over and groaned. He apologised, dressed hurriedly in the dark. He could hear her regular breathing from the bed, the suggestion of a swift return to sleep in the rhythm of her breath. She tasted a certain way in the mornings, and he thought about this as he zipped his rucksack and set it by the door. He didn't shower, but he did wash his face in the shared bathroom and flatten down his hair. Then he went back into her room to say goodbye. He kissed her on the cheek, but she was at least half asleep and his departure didn't seem to register.

Now the Young Man was on the coach. He sipped at a black coffee as he watched the road slip by, taking notice of the green metal signs stating the names of places and how far away they were, a concept of distance expressed succinctly in white numerals. Distinct from those other, unquantifiable distances that seemed to define his life: his girlfriend's increasing emotional distance; his own conscious desire to peel away from what remained of his family; the growing remoteness of the hopes he had once been naïve enough to cultivate for himself. And then the others, of course – the common distances all men lived with. Their distance from one another, from any real community which might last beyond the full-time whistle. From the millionaires who entertained them at weekends, the players whose wealth and success eclipsed the prospects of all their fans put together.

There was a man in the aisle seat beside the Young Man, but he had his headphones in and he wasn't saying anything. The Young Man didn't mind; he was feeling tired and unsociable, still bothered by how his girlfriend had been the night before. She had seemed fine while they were eating dinner, but then, when they settled in her bed to watch television on her laptop, she had gone quiet and brooding, the flick of a switch. The way she had snapped at him when he asked what was wrong, trying to comfort her. How she had said she was just stressed about her master's, and she didn't expect him to understand. And then, of course, she had shown him no warmth this morning before he tiptoed down the stairs to the front door, hoping he hadn't woken any of her housemates (strangers to her as much as to him) on the way out.

Now, with the hard shoulder scrolling beyond the window, the Young Man let his eyes unfocus and allowed the road to hypnotise him, the markings weaving here and splitting there, like dividing cells, roads merging and the hard shoulder shrugging to accommodate the slipway. They sucked him in, the patterns. He closed his eyes and saw a stranded family at the roadside, but now, in his imagination, he was the father, preparing to set off in search of an emergency phone, and his girlfriend was the mother whose hand was buried in the glove compartment. And their child was not a child at all but something else – something which had no name beyond the world of his dream, the logic of the semiconscious.

In his dream the Young Man felt the coach slowing, and then he realised he was not dreaming any more. They were far from home and pulling, already, into a car park. Behind him, empty cans clanked – that feeble, hollow sound of tin against tin – as they were gathered up and dropped into a bin bag. Someone else was drumming on a headrest, the tune to a familiar song, and others were singing along. The Young Man rubbed at his eyes, wondering how he had slept through the din.

As they were making their way to the designated away pub, the Young Man traded a few words with the other men and women who had been on the coach. They were almost all wearing club jerseys. They mostly favoured home kits, but some sported away strips from this season and from seasons in the recent past. Everyone in their group had a scarf, flashing green and yellow like ambulance markings, or else like an ironic pastiche of the colours of the Brazilian national team. The Young Man still did not feel like talking, but he didn't want to seem rude and so he joined in where he could.

The away pub, as advertised, was favourable to their custom. The travellers were happy to spend their time and money there until they were ready to go to the stadium. The Young Man felt his worries grow lighter as he drank, and in time they fell away completely. He was talking freely, now, about the Irishman, recounting the hat-trick of the previous week in great detail, even though the man he was talking to had been there at the ground and had seen it with his own eyes.

When it was time to set off for the stadium they walked easily through those exotic streets. A few jeers from rival fans but nothing serious. The Young Man messaged his girlfriend as he walked, writing that he was almost at the ground and was having a good time. He said he was thinking of her.

Thanks, she wrote, in response. She was, evidently, awake. She did not acknowledge the strangeness of the previous night, the somnolent hostility of that morning, and neither did he. By the time the team sheets came out, he had forgotten all about it.

In the past fortnight or so, something of an injury crisis had emerged; two goalkeepers were named among the substitutes. The Finn was fit enough to join them on the bench but not fit enough to start. It meant the Irishman, as expected, would be leading the line, aiming for a repeat of his previous performance. The Kosovan was out wide. The Norwegian kept his place, although everyone knew he was just making up the numbers. He would go back to his parent club at the end of the season, and then the fans wouldn't have to see him in their kit ever again. He might never again play in England, for that matter.

Today the Norwegian, as so often, proved to be the weak link. They were overwhelmed in midfield, and it was there that the game was lost, a flurry of first-half goals sealing their fate. Come the interval, the Young Man feared the game might finish, as the cliché goes, with a cricket score.

The only positive was that the Irishman had another good game, and although they were already three down by that point, he clawed back a good consolation goal in the second half. It was a well-taken strike from just inside the box, and the Young Man watched the Irishman run to the corner flag in celebration. He slapped the flag and then pulled up to welcome the embraces of his teammates: none so enthusiastic as him, given the score. The Irishman had come from nowhere, and now he had truly cemented himself in the consciousness of his city. His name, by this point in the season, was even being mentioned in wider circles. Further testament to his ascension: according to the official stats, he appeared now in some 8.6 per cent of all fantasy football teams – up from 0.1 per cent at the start of the season. Still, his goal was not enough to salvage the game. It merely salved the scoreline, sparing the fans' embarrassment and denying the opposition the gloss of a clean sheet. In the away end, damp applause met the full-time whistle, and the travelling fans did not linger long before they rolled up their flags and started to trudge down the steps.

The Young Man looked at his phone as he was leaving the ground. There was another message from his girlfriend.

I'm sorry, she wrote. I didn't mean to be short with you yesterday, but I'm really struggling with all this. Sorry about the score as well.

There was also a text from the Old Man. Bad luck today, his message read.

They would have a lot to discuss at the next home game, the Young Man thought. But first, he had to get back. And he still owed a reply to his girlfriend. He supposed the Irishman never had to deal with these problems, never doubted himself in times like these.

But the Young Man was wrong. Because while he did not know it, the Young Man was both profoundly different and profoundly similar to his newest idol. The Irishman had nobody so close in his life; he found it hard to trust that people didn't want to be with him just because he was going to be rich and famous and was contracted to a football club – even if that club was straggling at the wrong end of the table. The Irishman and the Young Man shared, then, the same fears about their suitability for love, even if the reasons could not have been more different. The Irishman feared he had too much about him; the Young Man feared he did not have enough. Yet in other ways, the distances between the Young Man and the Irishman were that much greater.

Tonight, the Irishman would fly back to their city. The Young Man, on the other hand, had his seat booked on the supporters' coach. After the rigours of ninety minutes in the stands, the Young Man was tired and his foot hurt, and he planned to shut his eyes for a while on the way back. The Irishman, exhausted to his bones and beset by professional anxieties unimaginable to the Young Man, also hoped for the sweet oblivion of sleep. They had many different dreams, these young men, but some of them were the same. They wanted to stay in the division, for one thing. They wanted to be loved, for another.

25

THE RIVER

THEY WERE DOWN BY the river, the Young Man and his girlfriend. It was cold but not unbearably so, and beneath their jackets they wore matching football jerseys. His jacket was hanging open so that the yellow fabric of the shirt and the name of the sponsor was visible. Her jacket was fully fastened. She had a scarf around her neck.

He didn't think she had been herself at the match. It was a shame, really, because it had been a good game. They had all played well – even, to the stadium's great surprise, the Norwegian. Rarely all season had the eleven seemed so cohesive; the trick, now, was to find a way to do it every week, to overcome the inconsistency that was coming to define the club and the German's style of management.

The Young Man and his girlfriend had come here, to the path beside the river, straight after the whistle had blown on that pleasing performance. They were here because she said there were things they needed to talk about. They were not yet talking, however. They were just walking, in silence. He was waiting for her to speak, but she seemed lost in some interior world, a space forever closed to him. She reached out with one hand and trailed her fingers along the sparse bushes which lined the path. She picked a leaf and rubbed it between her fingers, then she raised her fingers to her nose. She held this pose for a second before dropping the leaf, sacrificing it to the breeze. The Young Man, walking closer to the river, looked out at the water, at the half-ruined watchtower looming beyond, a relic from their city's rich history.

The Young Man had a sour, almost metallic, taste in his mouth – a taste he associated with drinking lager too fast. It was a sensation which often lingered after a pint or two at the ground. Today he hadn't had much, but it was enough. Bringing his girlfriend to the football – their first home game together – had been sufficient to give him a buzz all by itself. He had been excited about the game ever since he bought her ticket, the seat beside his.

The Old Man was always to the right of the Young Man, but the seat to the Young Man's left did not belong to any season ticket holder. This unclaimed seat was taken by someone different each game, a succession of strangers – casual supporters, many of them – to whom the Young Man rarely spoke. But this week, the Young Man had been able to book the second seat for himself, so he had two together and the Old Man to his side.

The Young Man had been excited to show his girlfriend around the ground, to introduce her to the Old Man and induct her into their rituals. He had assumed she would get swept up in the atmosphere and enjoy the game, but she smiled only weakly when they went one-up. She suffered the Young Man to throw his arm around her as the goal music came on, but after a moment of close contact she shrugged him off and sat down again. Clearly, she possessed an immunity to the spells of the stadium, that place where the Young Man felt the elusive pull of human connection at its strongest (barring, perhaps, his bed during those nights he spent with her). Her attitude had made it difficult to enjoy the second half. And because she was there, he hadn't spoken to the Old Man as much as usual.

It had been a mistake to bring her, but this truth revealed itself to the Young Man only now, only as the two of them were walking by the river with the smells of water and damp grass hanging in the air. It was so quiet here, especially after the stadium. She said, at last, that she hadn't been able to hear herself think back there; everything was too loud, too disordered.

That whole experience stressed me out, she added.

But I was there with you, the Young Man said. I wouldn't have let anything bad happen. And you were fine last time.

It's not about that, she said. It was just all too much. Did you not notice that I was watching the clock for almost all the second half?

Oh, he said. I'm sorry. And then he let his gaze drift back to the river.

There was nobody on the water, not this time of year. The willows – cousins, perhaps, of those which grew near his flat – had been stripped back by the cold, and the limbs hung weak and naked in the water. Gravel crunched underfoot with each step. He looked at her.

I don't understand what's wrong, he said. What are we doing here?

She sighed. None of this is easy for me, she said. I'm sorry.

Right, he said. Then, I don't get it.

Here, sit down.

They were almost at the watchtower, and they stopped at the bench opposite. The bench was slightly damp, and the cold started to creep through the Young Man's trousers as soon as he sat down. He saw now that he was holding a twig, something snapped from a tree or a bush. He did not remember, but he supposed he must have broken it off somewhere on the way – subconsciously emulating her, perhaps. Now he bent the twig in two and discarded the pieces without thinking.

They sat and shared the view of the water, the watchtower. The way the watchtower had been built, its age and its perfect roundness, made the Young Man think again of chess, a giant rook rising before him on the board of his life. He did not have many memories of his father, but one of his earliest recollections was of a travel chess set, his father trying to teach him what each of the tiny plastic pieces did. He remembered his father's frustration, his inability to understand that his boy was yet much too young to grasp the rules. He had just wanted to play with the pieces as if they were obscure action figures, lining them up in new formations and knocking them down.

And then the Young Man thought of the Old Man, wondering whether he had ever played chess, what he would be like as a teacher of the rules. The Young Man had not seen a real set for years; whenever he did, he was reminded of his father, cheap plastic between a child's fat fingers. Then his girlfriend said something: the cold, the tower, her. He asked her to repeat herself; he didn't think he had heard her right.

The tower was curved because square edges presented weaknesses for cannonballs. It was built from the same material as the castle and the cathedral, whose grounds began not far from here. This was an old part of the city. (Rooks moved as far as you wanted them to in a straight line, no diagonals; castling was a means of leaping your king sideways beyond a rook.)

He had heard her right the first time.

26

AFTER HER

Kick-off had been moved for television coverage, again. The studio voyeurs had developed a taste for the relegation battle. It meant the Young Man would have to take a half day and make the long coach journey to the game on Friday afternoon. He didn't mind too much. But it did feel sometimes as if the people who decided the TV schedule didn't care about the fans. He supposed it was just indicative of the direction the game had gone. Or the direction it had been taken, in many cases.

The good thing about the Friday-night kick-off was that the Young Man now had something to look forward to after work. He would not be seeing his girlfriend at the weekend because she was no longer his girlfriend. She had always had her problems, but now she had asserted her belief that he was the only one who benefited from their relationship; for her, it was just dredging up difficult emotions and making life harder. She said she was sorry; she had been put on a waiting list for a therapist, so she could start to work through it all. But despite how many messages he sent, how many changes he proposed or how many imagined futures he invoked, they could not be together.

The Young Man wouldn't get back until long after midnight, but that didn't matter. He had nothing to do over the weekend, so he could easily catch up on the lost sleep. And it was a big game for the club, another dogfight on the cusp of the drop zone. There was the potential for points. And with the Irishman in such a rich vein of form, there would probably be goals. At both ends, most likely.

The club had finally given in to the insistent demands of the younger supporters, and from now on, they were letting a prominent fan group bring their own drum to the games. Some of the fans thought that would change everything, but as he stared at his screen – the light seeming to press against the surface of his eyes, slipping over the membranous hemispheres and into the cavities behind them – the Young Man wasn't so sure.

The thing about the Young Man's work was this: he could tolerate it, so long as he didn't think about it. It was when he slowed down enough to process it that the problems started. Then the discontent would surge from somewhere deep inside of him, tightening his chest and quickening his pulse. He would be overcome by the feeling that he was stuck on his axis, unable to advance and with nowhere to retreat to, no hope of becoming something better (moving forward one space per turn, or two if it's the pawn's first move of the game, and always taking one space diagonally). But so long as he never allowed himself to truly experience his workdays as something that happened to him, everything would be fine, as it had been – mostly – for years. Each day passed; it always did. It was only a problem when the day's passing struck him in a tangible sense, and then the discontent would come back.

Maybe once every few months, a thought would come along these lines: human beings evolved from single-celled organisms on the only planet known to support intelligent life. Then we were animals, concerned only with the essentials of animal survival: sustenance and reproduction. Hundreds of thousands of years passed. Ever since the evolution of the species, and for an unfathomable amount of time previously, the sun has been cooling and expanding and dying, because time is a real force which exerts its influence upon us all. Civilisations rise and fall; men have set foot on the moon, and yet we still have no idea where our consciousness goes when we sleep. And now, owing to the continued centralisation of political power – the risks heightened astronomically by the current war – two or three senile and aggressive old men have inherited the power to destroy all human civilisation; the lucky ones will die in the blasts, and the survivors will be bequeathed the pangs of a diminished world, whatever is left behind. And one day, you too will die, the thought goes, and you are sitting here typing numbers into a spreadsheet as if that day will never come.

This kind of reasoning, the logic of a Great Resignation, deeply unsettled the Young Man. So it was important, every day, to make sure his workdays were filled – or else reason might find its way in. If the Young Man recognised, or thought he recognised, the onset of this line of thinking, it was essential that he crowded it out before it could take root. He would do this by getting up and making a coffee. Or he would put on his headphones and listen to his father's music. Or he would type, into a search bar, the name of his football club. He would see what the papers were saying, and he would look at the league table and work through permutations in his head. What he couldn't do was indulge that kind of thinking, because then he would find himself printing off the resignation letter he had already drafted and emailed to himself (its composition born of a frenzied evening months ago, the sum of a summer workday in which he had allowed those same thoughts to overwhelm him).

That was why it was fortunate, in a way, that there was a game tonight. It gave the Young Man something to look forward to; it proved there were still good things in his life, even if she was no longer one of them. And even if the awareness of the impossible wealth of his heroes on the pitch only made him more inclined to shred everything and start over in a futile, desperate attempt to be more like them, the boyish men who had never grown up, who kicked balls for a living and who never had to worry about what might come next. The Young Man watched the training videos the club put out every week, the men talking and laughing as they ran their drills. It was hard work, of course; all of them were at their physical peak, living clean and with an absolute commitment to what they did. But still, their luck was ludicrous.

It was play as work, professional football, an impossible concept of joy-for-hire which seemed so out of place in an economy which valued job satisfaction not at all, an economy obsessed with measurable gains. But how could you measure the beauty of a perfect volley, the heart-in-mouth exuberance of a goal-line clearance? The Young Man supposed this was not a question for him so much as for his idols, those young men with perfect houses and beautiful wives and children whose fathers were heroes and whose futures were already secure, forever. Men, in short, to whom it would never occur to ask themselves whether they were wasting their lives, because the answer was so obvious.

27

MEMORY

JUST AS THEY WERE threatening to string together some form and break free of the relegation battle, the international break appeared on the horizon. It had crept up on them, as it often did; the break was always closer than anyone realised. It had certainly seemed to the Young Man that this great run of fixtures would stretch forever ahead, and then suddenly they were playing their last home game, the penultimate fixture, before the pause. When they next played in the city, it would be spring proper. It would probably be raining, as it was today.

The Young Man, looking out the window at the wet surface of the road, pulled a home jersey over his hooded jumper. He had lent his umbrella to his ex-girlfriend weeks ago; she had yet to give it back, so he set off into the rain without it. At the bridge, where he had so often seen the beggar in times gone by, he stopped for a moment and watched the rain falling.

Droplets, like bullets, sent ripples running across the surface of the river. He felt and heard the gentle tapping of raindrops atop his hood. The trees would be budding soon, he supposed.

The Young Man had read a local news story, the previous week, about someone who had jumped into this same river from a bridge out of town. He was thinking about this as he made for the stadium, taking his usual route past the market. There was a beggar there – a different one – beneath the awning of a closed stall that, weekday lunchtimes, sold empanadas to office workers. The beggar stopped the Young Man, asked him for money. The Young Man had no change, but he bought the beggar a sandwich and a drink from the paper shop on the corner. Losing her, it seemed, had made him benevolent. He didn't want to be late, though, so he didn't linger. It was fair to say that he was doing better, at least, than last weekend, when he had drunk too much after the game, the journey home a sickly blur, and had woken to a message threating to block his number if he didn't stop calling her. He feared where his mind might take him next. (Would he forget the smell of her shampoo and the texture of her skin, that ladder of scars beneath the peach hairs on her arm? Would he forget, also, what it was about him that had made him worthy of her love?)

•

Across town, the Old Man was stepping into the rain for the second time that day. Unlike the Young Man, he had his umbrella with him, the handle cold against his bare hands. And unlike the Young Man, he no longer dressed in club colours for the games. The only visible sign of his allegiance was the yellow and green scarf about his neck (his pinprick tattoos being hidden beneath layers and their meanings indecipherable to anyone but him, regardless). Still, he got a cheer from a group of fans as he walked past the riverside pub, the cheap one nearest the ground. He thought the shouting was for him, at least, though he couldn't imagine why.

The pub was brimming with home supporters, many of them drinking for warmth against the rain. It was the typical matchday crowd. The Old Man had not been inside that pub for many years, but he knew it was a football pub; away fans weren't allowed in. There had been one or two fights before that rule was introduced, but it wasn't really that sort of place any more. Nor was theirs that sort of club.

Men gathered around the picnic benches outside the pub, clusters of drinkers in the tiled garden that overlooked the river. Football fans, like football players, are superstitious by nature, and some said you could predict the scoreline on any given matchday by noting how the waterfowl were grouped. Two swans close by and one goose at a distance, say, meant a home win, two goals to one. But the birds kept from the open today. They were probably all seeking shelter at the riverbank. The drinkers, too, huddled close beneath the parasols, standing because the benches were damp. They drank lager from plastic cups. Rainwater was getting in, but nobody cared. The pub, inside, smelled like wet; the Old Man knew this to be true without going in himself.

The Old Man no longer drank, but the environment of the pub was not so alien to him. He understood the nature of these places, where England resides in its truest and most concentrated form. It seemed to the Old Man that the truth of England and what it was had been forgotten by the people who wrote his newspapers and his laws, but it did not matter much. He would not burden his children with the inheritance of this diminished England, because he had no children. All that mattered, for now, was that the team finished strongly before all their momentum was swept away by the international break. Then it would be the time of a different England – one the Old Man could no longer recognise. But first, there was the football, that teeming, therapeutic distraction.

The two men – Old and Young – soon met on the terrace, at their adjacent seats. Two men looking, as ever, for a sense of belonging and purpose they had so far only been able to find at the ground. They greeted one another, and the Old Man asked the Young Man how he had been.

You know, said the Young Man, an equivocal tilt of the head, a grimace. How about you?

I'm much the same, said the Old Man. What's getting you down now?

The Young Man shrugged. Just life, he said. He forced a smile.

Something to do with that girl of yours? The Old Man took the silence for confirmation. Was I right the first time? he asked. Didn't I say?

The Young Man laughed. The stadium announcer stated over the music that the players were coming out for their warm-ups. The rain was drumming against the corrugated metal roof of the terrace: a relentless, reverberating, pelting noise. It was how it must sound to go insane, the Young Man thought. But for now, he simply laughed. He laughed and said, I'm going in for a pint.

Wait a second, said the Old Man.

What?

The Old Man offered one of his thin smiles: dry lips, deep grooves beside the eyes. Take it from an old man, he said. Whatever it is, you'll get over it.

Thanks, said the Young Man. I was serious about the pint though.

The Old Man stood so the Young Man could pass. He looked to the pitch, where the players were getting soaked in the warm-up. The Dutchman came over to applaud those fans already in their seats. His shirt was stuck to his chest, and his hair came down over his forehead like it had been plastered on. The Young Man shuffled by, blocking the view for a moment, and then he was off down the aisle. He went a few steps before he stopped and turned around.

Do you want a coffee? he asked. That magnanimity again, born of selfish grief. Like he was bereaved, the way he was going about.

No, thank you, said the Old Man. He sat back down and returned his gaze to the Dutchman. It occurred to the Old Man only as he saw the goalkeeper tightening the straps on his gloves that he had, for once, forgotten his own. The rain came still, and in the deluge the Old Man imagined a letter drifting from a balcony, released from the disbelieving grip of a gloveless hand. He saw it catching the rain, falling faster until it hit the ground. He saw it turning to mulch against the asphalt, ink smudged beneath boots, all words washed away by the coming storm. Then he looked back to the Dutchman and reminded himself why he was here. This was a conscious choice he was making – to lose himself in the football, in something he cared about. The alternative was unthinkable: becoming lost in the nothingness instead, in the practicalities of age and illness. In the websites of private clinics and the profiles of local nurses and care assistants, bank statements and powers of attorney, articles and information leaflets which were supposed to reassure him that there might be a few more good years left to him, that they might both retain their independence for the better part of a decade. It amounted to a passive ending for a man who feared his final years would be defined by passivity, who was desperate to take a stand against time itself without really knowing how one went about it or whether it was a fight anyone could honestly hope to win.

28

MILES AWAY

The whistle blew; it was full-time. The Young Man, in the stands of a distant ground, raised his hands above his head to applaud the team. The others in his part of the ground, separated from the home supporters by a few columns of covered seats, did likewise. The travelling players – spent, satisfied shells of themselves – lumbered over to clap the fans, the Young Man among them, who had come all this way. The home players made for the dugout.

Stewards in hi-vis jackets were arranged around the block of away fans. They put their bodies between the fans and the pitch as well as interceding between the away fans and the home fans on either side. Many of the stewards were overweight, there only for show. They were no fighting force. They all looked bored and yet strangely wary at the same time, although there was no real chance of anything kicking off – not on a day like today. The home fans were already pouring down the steps towards the exits; the away fans stayed behind in jubilant spirits.

That distinction – home and away – was so charged, the way the Young Man saw it. Home was a loaded word, comfort and safety; away was a place nobody wanted to be. And it mattered, this distinction. It marked out the fault lines of the crowd, the allegiance of the fans like a split personality within the hivemind of the football stadium. It was the stewards' job to keep the two from mixing. There were police officers all around the ground too, and everyone knew it was these men – and not the stewards – who wielded the real power, the power of the state against the individual as well as the power to eject and ban, to take away the sport which meant so much to so many.

Because while you could theoretically fall out of love with football, it was more likely that football would fall out of love with you. A stadium ban could end the affair for years or for life, the football authorities and the police and the clubs lining up against troublesome fans, denying them their passion. Disregarding complex social problems – questions of masculinity and violence and the nihilism and emptiness of modern life – by simply neutering those who could not coexist peacefully with the game. It did not happen often, but it happened. And it was always easy to pass new laws, no matter how ludicrous, when it was only football fans they affected. Already it was illegal to drink alcohol in view of the pitch, and this had been the case for as long as the Young Man had been going. Nor was it legal to watch a three p.m. Saturday kick-off on television or online – arbitrary rules designed to maximise profit, to bleed off excess passions. But these concerns could wait, the Young Man supposed. For now, he owed it to himself to try to inhabit this happy moment, to check those wandering thoughts whose leash had only become longer in the weeks of her absence.

The Young Man looked past the ranks of stewards to the pitch beyond. The players were almost level with the stewards now. This was as close as they usually came to the fans. Some unwritten rule – or perhaps it had even been codified somewhere – seemed to prevent the players from touching the men in the stands. This rule was contravened only in moments of intense joy and triumph, and while today's result was a good one, it was not enough to justify intermingling between the two factions: players and fans, kings and pawns, performers and their masters. Which way round was it really?

The Kosovan had come off the bench today, and he had played well. He was a cult hero, praised for his power and speed and his ready sense of humour in the heavily edited interviews the club released on social media. He looked now to the mass of fans, who had started singing one of their new songs, the beat kept by the drummer in the back of the stand. The Kosovan grinned and started dancing, clapping in time with the drum. A pair of supporters in the front row were holding aloft a Kosovan flag, and now the Kosovan noticed them, surprised to be confronted with his national symbol so far from home. He smiled and waved to the men, and then he took off his shirt and tossed it to one of them. Pure muscle beneath the GPS vest, like a sports bra, which the players all had to wear so their stats could be tracked.

A second later, something similar happened with the Finn. He noticed a young boy, scarcely ten years old, holding a piece of cardboard. The Young Man could not see from where he was standing, but he knew that on the other side of the cardboard would be a handwritten message asking for the Finn's shirt. The Finn duly took off his shirt and balled it up, tossing it underarm through a gap between two stewards. The boy caught it, dropping his sign in the excitement. The boy's father shouted his gratitude, and the Finn nodded, meeting the man's eyes for a moment. The Finn was not a character in the same way as the Kosovan; he did not have much of a personality when the ball was not at his feet. But the fans didn't mind. The Finn was their captain and their top scorer, and now the Argentinian was gone he was undoubtedly their best player. The fans cheered and sang his name and waited until all the players had turned and crossed the field, heading back to the tunnel. The German lingered for a moment to clap the travelling faithful, something he had always done after away games and something which had always endeared him to the supporters.

When the German finally waved goodbye, the Young Man reached into his pocket to check his phone. He had not been thinking about it during the match, but now it struck him that he had another long journey ahead. The one person he wanted to talk to had not messaged out of the blue to tell him it had all been a mistake and that she was sorry for breaking his heart. All he had was a message from his mother, asking whether he had enjoyed the game and if he had made plans to visit any time soon, like he had said he would at the funeral.

The Young Man turned to the man next to him and said it felt good to be pulling away from the relegation zone at last.

That's a good point for us, the stranger said.

A really good point, said the Young Man. Then they fell into silence, thoughts scored by the steady beating of the drum behind them.

The Young Man's city was not near anywhere. Nobody ever passed through; it was a destination and nothing less. It meant there were no easy away games, no games close to home bar the home games. But the Young Man would miss the football, even the coach journeys, during the international break. A fortnight stretched ahead, barren days in which all Englishmen, as they sang their tired anthem, became patriots and theists and defenders of the monarch (the king being able to move one square in any direction, the game lost when he is taken). It was funny, the Young Man thought, what sport could do to you. Football, in particular. And particularly in a place like his.

•

The Young Man may have only travelled for the football, but at least it got him out of the city. The Old Man, for his part, would have given almost anything to experience such variety, so many new places. It had been a long time since the Old Man had gone anywhere. Dreams of the coast, even, had become as remote and unlikely as interstellar travel. He could not discount the possibility that he would never leave the city again.

The Old Man had watched the match on television, hands clenching into fists as the Finn's late equaliser was called into doubt by a lengthy VAR check. But the Kosovan, who had supplied the assist, was adjudged to be onside after all, and so the goal had stood. An excellent point, salvaged late in a difficult game. But it was the break now, and that meant no more club football for a couple of weeks. He, too, would miss it.

The summer absence was bad enough, but at least the football was gone for so long in the off-season that you started to get used to it. To the Old Man, the international breaks felt like more of an imposition; it wasn't fair to play continually for months and then break off the flow so abruptly – not now they had finally found some consistency.

It was the schedulers, he knew. They had no regard for the fans. And the way he had come to see it, international football was a pale imitation of club football. Even though he had been alive for England's greatest triumph – even though he knew how international success tasted, how it could galvanise a nation of tens of millions – he shared the Young Man's distrust of the national team in its current guise.

The manager of the national team often came in for criticism from fans of club football. After every tournament exit, they railed against his innate conservatism, the cautiousness of his selections. And besides, the Old Man had chosen his club; his country had been chosen for him. Although he recognised even that was not strictly true – not when his club had been passed down the way it had. And even if his father had not been a fan, the accident of his birth in a one-club city would have established his support as an obvious default.

Today the Old Man's mind was particularly active, brimming with such pointless recollections and petty grievances against the world. He had been wondering, as the clock ticked towards ninety, how many games he had watched in his lifetime and how many remained for him to watch, whether all his life would boil down to goals and points. What, he wondered, would be the aggregate score of his existence? And what of his wife's aggregate? And then – the idea of it lurching out of the grass of the pitch, through the screen, almost – if he were to die before her, what would she do without him?

The Old Man had tried his best to avoid this particular worry, had avoided, until now, following this line of reasoning to its logical conclusion. For a moment – even as the ball was passed to the Kosovan, who cut to the byline and whose cross landed at the frantic feet of the onrushing Finn, square in front of goal, wiping out the score and adding another to the Old Man's lifetime aggregate – fear gripped him so completely that his expression remained impassive as the net bulged with the equaliser.

The goal meant the opposition's lead had all been for nothing; the equaliser erased all gains and effectively, despite the efforts of those twenty-two men and all the fans, reset the game to zero, the match circling all the way round to its starting point. The whole game, as he suddenly saw it, was an exercise in the absurd.

The Old Man's wife looked over at him, waiting for him to register the goal. It came a second later, the awareness. He smiled at her and said the shot had been well taken, though the Finn had only scuffed at it and all the beauty, really, had been in the Kosovan's inch-perfect cross. His wife said nothing, although the truth of his worry was reflected momentarily in the black of the television screen, into whose darkness he looked and saw himself: an old man staring at an old man.

In such conditions, under such rules, the Old Man realised no aggregate could ever matter. All you could do was play while you still could, with no regard for stoppages or extra time or penalties, even. As he watched his players celebrating

– miniature figures like the approximations of living, thinking men on the television screen – the Old Man told himself that there was no choice but to take life as it came, just as you had to take the matches as they came. Even the bloody internationals.

•

And later that night, as the Old Man slept, the Young Man looked up from his phone and felt the coach vibrating beneath him. He turned to the window and saw a motorway sign looming in the darkness beyond his bewildered reflection.

He knew then that his home city – and with it, his own retreat into sleep – was yet miles and miles away. All he could do was close his eyes and wait. In his mind he tried the old trick of reliving the goal over and over, trying to recapture the ecstasy of the moment, the joy of all those away fans. But these images were soon crowded out by thoughts of her. He tried to remember what it was that she had so cherished in him, what it was that might, one day, make another feel the same.

And beneath this, he too was searching for meaning, for reason, even if he didn't know it; he, too, was pushing up against an uncaring absurdity as he sought answers to his worries. But first there was the journey home, the pull of sleep at the end of it, and the motorway signs flaring at intervals in the darkness, closing the distance from home and from her even as time worked its influence in the opposite direction. Because every passing second carried him further away from the knowledge, tangled up in those thoughts of her – knotted among his sadness and lust and frustration – that he had deserved another person's love and would, one day, deserve to be loved again.

29

FAITH

HOME, A CITY OF BLACK FLINT and blue plaques. A place where time hangs heavy in the eaves of the churches; a place of chipped flagstone and sparse thatch and gravestones rising like milk teeth in every ragged shred of grass they can find. They say this is the most complete medieval city in all of England; they say Hitler ordered the Luftwaffe not to bomb the cathedral because it is an architectural treasure.

The Young Man didn't know about any of that. But he was as capable as any heartbroken young man of seeing deeper meanings wherever he looked, of being almost overcome by the world's fleeting, everyday beauty. The more ephemeral, the better: light skipping across a car bonnet; the laugh of a wetsuited paddleboarder, the first of the year, as he took to the water; the veins of a young leaf, translucent in the sun. These things moved him in ways he had never been moved before. In those moments sadness and joy stirred together, a heightened awareness of what was lovely and all the more so because it could never last, because he would never be able to articulate why he was so moved. And still he hoped that her name would appear on his phone; he imagined her writing that it had all been a big joke, sorry, April Fool!

From his apartment, few belongings and bare walls, the Young Man set off much too early for the game just so he had an excuse to take in the day. It was cool but bright, the sun clear and crisp in the sky. He was comfortable in the training top he wore above black trousers and running shoes, though he followed his consultant's advice and never ran anywhere.

Memories came back to him as he walked slowly down the street, waiting for his foot to wake up and fill with fresh blood and for the pain to subsequently numb, as it almost always did. He had been playing football when it all started: a double fracture, and he had deserved it, in his mind, for pulling out of a fifty-fifty challenge at the last moment. It was a bad break, but at the time he had walked home through gritted teeth, assuming it was just a sprain. He only learned later that he had a hereditary disposition to injuries of this kind, and that was why the bones had fused in a way no bones ought to fuse. Hence the onset of his disease and hence his inability to ever play football again. Hence his relegation to the stands for the rest of his life.

The Young Man still walked tentatively and with the trace of a limp, a biomechanical signature that made him appear always slightly off camber. The pain was slow to numb today, so he walked on the grass beside the pavement, flatter and gentler terrain. He knew the cobbled lanes would do him no good, so he took a longer route to the stadium, following the path along the knotted river. He gave himself over to the river's beauty as he walked its tortuous course: past the pubs with their paddleboards to let and through the garth to the arts university and the playhouse, the cathedral grounds.

Although he was not religious, the Young Man enjoyed the ecclesiastical flourishes for which his city was known. Churches were everywhere, and each gathered about itself a distinct aesthetic. If this were a city on the continent, he supposed, people would be lining up to photograph the ubiquitous churches and the lanes they framed. But it was not. And they didn't. Other things marked this place as different from the continent, too. The war had not come here, for one, and yet the ripples it caused, the shock to the economy, seemed worse here than almost anywhere else.

The past few years had sharpened everyone's awareness of these things. Supply chains were no longer abstract concepts, and rationing was more than a footnote from history. People like the Young Man, people who had been paying attention, knew how thin the curtain was which separated society from reality and how it felt to look beyond that curtain. Although he now understood, also, that it was human nature to be shocked by sudden, sad things and then to move on with your life, to be so consumed by your own worries that there was no room for anything else. That was certainly how he had been since she had left him, lurching from one beautiful thing to another, allowing himself to become hung up on the state of the world only in the brief interludes between. Knowing that if he let himself steep too long in his obsessions, he might never come out of them. His work had taught him, already, how to push aside truths that were not conducive to daily life. At the supermarket, for example, he had seen a sign informing customers that their free school meal vouchers could not be exchanged for alcohol. He had known the logic of this information could only lead to dark places, and so he quickly packed his bag and moved on.

Would you like your receipt? the girl on the checkout had asked. But the Young Man had already turned away; his headphones were already in, and his mind was already elsewhere.

Now he tried to draw himself once more into the moment: club football was back, and he was on his way to a home game. The world was beautiful and good, even as it was ugly and cruel. And here was the river, shimmering in the sun. Buds and blossoms overhead, smells of fresh grass, of spring, in the air. In one direction, the river led to a national park. In the other, it came out across town, near the football stadium. The apex of it all, as the Young Man saw it: a cathedral in its own right.

Maybe it still sounds like an exaggeration, but really it isn't. Take the talk on social media; they were saying the club wanted to modernise its crest. When the rumours leaked, supposedly from within the club, the fans responded with a vehemence which proved, for them, the spirituality of this question. They were not against change, but they were opposed to change for the sake of change.

The Young Man understood their impulses well enough. He had been thinking about getting the crest tattooed, although he was going to hold off now until he knew for sure what it would look like next season. But it said something that for many of the fans the iconography of the club and the topography of their bodies were, in places, one and the same. It bespeaks a love not natural to men to have the symbology of a secular faith punched, point by point, into one's skin.

And none of this is to mention the street in the centre of town – the street named for the elms which had once grown there. They were long dead, victims of imported disease, and they would never grow again. But it made the Young Man laugh, on his walk to the stadium, to see the street sign and ask to himself where the elms had ended up, who had been hiding them away and to what end they had been stripped out; discarded, he supposed, in favour of something else.

30

THE RUN-IN

AND THIS IS WHY THE Young Man found it so strange – so strange and disquieting – to see what other places were really like. When he travelled to away games, he was often shocked at the spiritual impoverishment of the cities he visited. The stadiums were hollow places: inept, inert. They were deconsecrated churches, burial grounds with all the graves dug up. And the streets he walked were so sparse of beauty in comparison to those he knew. At the final trill of the whistle, he would become desperate to go home. He did not sing on the coach. He simply watched those same motorway signs from the window and counted down the distance to the city where he had left so much of himself behind.

It had only been in the past month or so that the beauty of those wise streets and the knowing river had become truly apparent to him. When he was away from them, he simply went through the motions. He drank the same beer in the same pubs as the other travelling fans, but he did not see the same gestalt in the bottom of his glass. And although he played his part before the game, cheering the line-up and singing all the right songs, the events of the pitch were secondary to his true concern: the ephemerality of everything he loved and the growing urge to do something about it.

This was a logic the Old Man understood well. If the Young Man had ever voiced these concerns, the Old Man might have turned to him and told him how lucky he was to have figured it out so young, when there was still time to make the necessary adjustments. But then again, perhaps the Old Man might have held to his lips a finger printed with ink and told the Young Man to stop distracting him from the game, the Irishman having won the ball in the air and the Finn through on goal and their keeper on his knees (arms outstretched) like the wild postulant of some forgotten order.

Either way, the Young Man was on his own today, the Old Man's travelling days long behind him. And so, without his neighbour and companion to talk to, he had to force himself to take in the game, to enjoy the feeling of being one up away from home, rubbing it in and spoiling everyone else's day and not feeling bad about it for a second.

The Finn had scored very early – too early, some might say – and they had been trying to defend this fragile lead ever since. Now, with the second half slipping by, they were making the most dangerous lead in football seem especially precarious.

For one, the Finn was clearly exhausted. Ever since the restart they had been playing it in the air for him, relying on his hold-up play, which had never been one of his strengths. The Irishman, who was more suited to that style of football, had been forced off at half-time with a knock. The men in the stands blamed the international break; the Irishman had been called up for the first time and had clearly aggravated something while he was away. They were a constant source of frustration, the breaks.

Further down the pitch, the Frenchman had been having a good game, but now he clashed heads with a rival midfielder and fell awkwardly to the turf. The young Englishman also looked like he was finished; he doubled over, winded, after hoofing the ball up-field and out of play. Medics ran on for the Frenchman, and from his vantage point in the stands the Young Man could see a physio holding up a hand to the midfielder's face, asking how many fingers he could see.

I don't like the look of this, said the stranger beside the Young Man. I don't think this lot have enough about them to hold on till the whistle. They don't have the minerals.

We have to find a way, the Young Man said. We need the points.

I know we do, said the stranger. I'm not denying that. I just don't think they have it in them.

After a few minutes of treatment, the magic sponge and some cold spray, the Frenchman let himself be walked off the pitch. The Englishman looked over to the dugout, gesturing that he wanted to come off as well. The board went up a moment later; the Englishman and the Frenchman went off. The Kosovan and the Norwegian came on. The Young Man sighed when he saw the Norwegian's number on the board. The Norwegian was no gamechanger, he knew.

It was soon clear that the Kosovan, fresh from the bench, was going to be their only outlet and their only real hope of killing off the game. He was tireless, as always, skipping over slide tackles and running the ball to the corner flag to give everyone else a chance to catch their breath. The problem with the Kosovan, and the reason he didn't always start, was that he couldn't finish. Everyone knew he was useless when he found himself in the box, under pressure; he could assist goals, but he didn't score them. The Finn was still getting into good positions, but the ball just wouldn't come to his feet. With ten minutes left, the Finn stopped pressing. Increasingly, it appeared as if they would have to defend their way to the final whistle.

Throughout this anxious second half, the Young Man's stare kept drifting to the scoreboard, where the elapsed minutes were tallied to the second. He watched the oversized clock tick by and willed the team to close out the game. It was important that they take at least a point home with them. They were safe in the table, for now, but nothing in this league was guaranteed. The international break hadn't helped. It had come at a bad time, when they were playing well, and stripped away all their momentum. They still needed a final clutch of points to make certain they would not get sucked into the relegation zone at the end of the season.

The fans knew that there was still plenty of time for their team to slip up – both in the context of the game and the season as a whole – and accordingly, a nervous energy started to rise in the away section. Could the players sense the anxieties of their fans? Were they responsible for what happened next? Either way, it was clear that the home crowd could pick up on the nervousness. The rival supporters fed off the worries of the Young Man and those around him, and soon the stadium was louder than ever, the home fans worked up and willing their team forward, pressure building by the minute. They thought they could smell blood, was what it was.

Minutes after an attacking change, the home side finally found a way through. A neat ball split the centre-halves, both notoriously slow on the turn, and found a fresh-legged young striker, who scored with his first touch. Curses and shouts rose from the away end; cheers came surging from every other corner of the ground. There was still time for the opposition to go on and win it, and as the Young Man watched the substitute striker pick the ball out of the net and sprint back to the centre circle, he realised that was what they would try to do.

Nobody knew for sure what relegation would mean, how the finances of the club were structured, but clearly tens of millions of pounds were at stake. If they went down, jobs and hope would be lost. Their best players, the young prospects like the Englishman and the Irishman and veterans like the Finn, would all leave. It wasn't clear, from the accounts, how long the club would be able to continue without the rights money and TV revenue from playing in this league. And if they didn't come straight back up, they risked being sucked into the maelstrom of the lower leagues – ruin compounding ruin, the hugeness of the stakes generating a certain gravity. Big clubs up north had been scooped out by relegation. Some had gone bust.

It was difficult for the Young Man to imagine what his life would be like without the club. The football was an anchoring presence; it kept him distracted. Although when the opposition found the winner – an own-goal by one of the exhausted centre-halves, born of a corner deep into stoppage time – the Young Man wished it were not so. The ball trickled across the line, the Dutchman having been wrong-footed, and the home fans erupted. The jeers seemed intensely personal, and they seemed to come from everywhere, from all around the ground as well as from inside the Young Man's skull. He was sure, for a moment, that he was alone against them all, lost to the well of inhospitable noise. Then he wished, surveying the distraught postures of the men in yellow, that he could find a way to live without distractions, were such a thing even possible. Or else he wished that he still had her, so he didn't have to rely so much for his happiness on a sport known for its cruelty and capriciousness. In that moment, the smug stadium announcer stated the own-goalscorer's name, the minute of the goal, and the home fans started singing even louder. On the pitch, by the dugouts, the substitute striker, whose corner had ultimately forced the winner, was being mobbed by teammates and coaches, hooked players in their huge coats running from the bench and unused subs in their training tops and bibs sprinting down the touchline to jump on his back. It was awful watching those strangers sharing in their moment, a moment made in the exclusion and misfortune of the Young Man and his team.

The stranger beside the Young Man exhaled loudly. We scored too early, he said. I fucking knew they didn't have it in them.

That'll be their confidence shot for the rest of the season, said another of the men.

The Young Man said nothing. He merely looked to the scoreboard in disgust, his misery the inverse of the home fans' joy, all beautiful things forgotten for the moment.

31

OPTIMISM

Something had snapped within the Young Man. He realised that, without being able to pinpoint quite when or how, but suspecting he knew why, he had crossed an internal Rubicon. His old coping strategies – his regimen of forced ignorance, of distracting himself with the football – were no longer working, and so he had resolved that the time had come for drastic action.

He stood, waiting, by the printer. There was a spooling noise and a flashing of lights, and then out came the letter. The paper was warm. He looked at his watch. A few hours yet until the weekend, but first he had to hand in the letter. They were playing at home; it was something to look forward to. But really, seriously, he had to get the letter out of the way first.

The Young Man's resignation letter had been waiting in his inbox for a long time. He always knew he would be grateful for it one day. It was like the cyanide pills which had once been carried by spies in case they were captured. Maybe, against the backdrop of the coming Second Cold War, they would again. For the Young Man, the letter was his own way out, a means of escape. Although with his meagre savings it wasn't clear where exactly he was escaping to; anywhere, he supposed, would be better than his present situation. The thought was cheering, and he found himself smiling as he re-read the words, the warmth of paper fresh from the printer comforting against his fingers.

What he really wanted to do, in that moment, was thank her. Because if it hadn't been for her, he doubted he would ever have found the courage to make this change. It was a big deal, what he was doing, like substituting your keeper before a cup-final shootout. And without the impetus of her breakup, he certainly wouldn't have thought to do this now, in the current climate, with times of shortages and suffering not far off, a difficult winter looming at the end of the year. But for now, he was happy, and it took all his restraint not to write her a message telling her as much.

The paper in his hands, its warmth slowly fading, prompted a sensory echo: her hand in his as they pushed through a train-station crowd, their big away day in the capital. The smoothness of her palm, just faintly slick where her nerves had got the better of her. From there, it was easy to make the leap to the badly bitten nails, the feel of those fine hairs on her arms, the way they caught the light, her laugh. And then the scars beneath the hairs, those tracts of ghost skin an inheritance from earlier days, and the way her moods could pivot drastically with only the slightest trigger: euphoria and dysphoria married in the same minute. He had to make allowances for her, he remembered, shaking off the memories before they got too deep into him. And yet he knew that, despite how it ended, she would not have begrudged him his happiness in this moment.

•

Matchday, and the Young Man celebrating his new-found freedom on the concourse. He was a little woozy when he emerged, at last, into the sunlight, concrete steps flaring harshly beneath his feet, the yellow of the seats a distinct provocation. He regretted not wearing a cap. He regretted, also, not having eaten earlier that day, but he was wise enough not to place his faith in any of the reheated and overpriced fare they sold inside the ground. He would simply have to push through.

You're looking chipper today, said the Old Man. He who knew all about pushing through, he who had endured a lifetime of it.

Thanks, said the Young Man. He grinned. Then he shucked off his jacket and dumped it in the fold of his seat. He shielded his eyes with his hand, surveying the pitch: various officials and staff buzzing around with their clipboards and radios and telephones. The Young Man smiling still, head swimming, acting like the whole scene was there just for him, arranged solely for his pleasure: the stadium and the staff and the fans and even the sunlight on his bare arms. Who did he think he was, that Young Man? Nelson? No matter, because now he lowered his hand and turned back to the Old Man.

How's things? he asked.

Same as ever, said the Old Man. But perhaps his exuberance

was catching, because today the Old Man smiled to show that this was not necessarily a bad state of being, not always.

Score?

I don't know. So long as we get something from this, I'll be happy. The Old Man shook his head. He said, Doesn't even matter how we go about it now, does it? So long as we don't get sucked in. Because if you ask me, it feels like it's going to be tighter at the end than anyone realises, and I don't know if we're really good enough to be in this league any more. The Old Man sighed. Still, he added, I think it would finish me off if we went down now, after the season we've been having.

The Young Man smiled; he had never known the Old Man say so many words at once. He wondered whether everything was richer in texture today because he had left his job. The music seemed to come crisper from the speakers; the moulded plastic of the seat felt harsher and more inhospitable than usual, even through the padding of his jacket. The players would be out any minute. They would line up, as they always did, and shake hands. The fans would sing. The Young Man knew well how it went.

As he watched the mouth of the tunnel, waiting for something to happen, he made a game of picturing the hourglass of his savings, money slipping like sand with each passing day. But he had to work his notice period first. He could worry about what might come next after he had caught his breath.

Then the announcer's voice came over the loudspeaker, stating that the players were in the tunnel; it was nearly time for kick-off, time to make some noise! The Young Man felt himself slipping back into the moment, a numbing comfort not dissimilar to sinking into a warm bath. He realised, then, that it might not even matter if he ran out of money. The team might be relegated by then, or else the war might escalate even further and suck in everyone else, the fate of the species in the hands of a few gamblers. This prospect did not unsettle him as it once had.

Some people were saying that energy rationing might be introduced on the continent. The Americans, meanwhile, were insisting that there was no blockade; there had never been a blockade. The significance of this was lost on the Young Man, newly jobless, who just trying to live while he was alive. That was his new philosophy. It was why he stood and belted out the club's song with such enthusiasm when the players came out. And yes, his exuberance was definitely catching; today the Old Man clapped his hands above his head and joined in the singing. They knew a couple more wins would keep them safe in the division. It was just a question of getting some momentum going again.

The Young Man sung throughout the first half. He didn't always sing so much at home games; he usually saved his voice for when they were playing away, when you had to bring the noise yourself because nobody else was going to sing for you. But today he was content to sing. The Old Man kept looking at the Young Man like something had gotten into him. He was not surprised when the Young Man rose unsteadily to his feet at half-time, announcing his intention to head back in for another pint or two. When the Young Man came back, he looked like he had been drinking something harder than that, and he almost tripped on the stairs on his way up. A steward was keeping an eye on him, as was the Old Man. But it didn't matter – not today. A quiet voice at the back his head told him he was only mortgaging his happiness from the following days and weeks, but when he sang louder, the voice went away. He knew he had to enjoy moments like these while he could.

In the second half, the away fans thought they had scored. Indeed, the ball was in the net, but the linesman had his flag up; their forward had been offside. The Young Man had looked straight to the linesman as the ball went in, but the away fans, in their jubilation, seemed not to notice. They were granted a few seconds of exuberant celebration before they realised the goal would not stand. At this, the mass of away fans quietened suddenly, and the home fans started cheering instead, delighting in the scratching of the goal and the embarrassment of the opposition.

The Young Man nudged the Old Man and pointed to the away block. A grotesquely fat man in the front row had taken off his shirt, but with the goal chalked out he was now busy putting it back on. He became briefly entangled in the sleeves, a knot of polyester and surplus flesh and, the Young Man suspected, shame. Jeers started on the terrace, a fresh chant directed towards the away fans.

The Young Man inhaled deeply. What a day, he said. And it was true that he was enjoying himself, that he had allowed his worries to be smothered by the match, the way the Dutchman rushed out now to smother a fresh attack, diving on the ball at the feet of the opposition forward and earning his warm applause from the stands. Things couldn't be all that bad, the Young Man supposed, if the football was still going ahead.

But at the other end of the pitch, momentarily unseen by the Young Man, the Finn was rolling around and holding his ankle. Something had happened off the ball. The German was at the border of the technical area, shouting at the referee and the fourth official and anyone else who would listen, telling them to stop play, pointing frantically at the Finn. The Young Man clapped his hands and joined in another song. He let the music rise all around him, felt rather than heard the beat of the drum, and just for a moment he forgot where he was. It seemed nothing could spoil his day. But then the board went up, and the Finn was stretchered off the field, and a late flurry of goals saw them lose three-nil.

32

REALISM

THE YOUNG MAN WITHDREW his notice on Monday. A weekend was all it took. That foul hangover and then, mixed up with the pain in his foot and the tightness in his chest, the crushing sense that he had made a mistake and might forever struggle to come back from it. He felt like those away fans who had thought they had scored, only for reality to come crashing down a moment later. But the Young Man didn't have what those fans had, which was the reassurance of three points at the end of it, vindication for the embarrassment and heartbreak suffered along the way. And then he was back talking to his boss and apologising for the inconvenience and saying it wouldn't happen again. He had put on a tie and everything. He felt like a dickhead, his inadequacy laid bare in his search history: how to tie a tie; easiest tie knots for beginners; simple tie knot tutorial. (And wasn't this the kind of thing his father should have taught him? This, along with how to shave and how to be around women and how to make something of your life? What had his father given him, really, he had to ask, besides a football team and a few rock albums?)

There was another match, at least, at the end of the long week. Another marathon coach journey, another city the Young Man had never seen before and would only see between the car park and the pub and the stadium and back again. People like him, wearing the same jersey and bound by allegiance to the same club, to something bigger than themselves – a miracle, really, in this age of atomisation. Football was the one language everyone could speak – instinctively, in most cases. How else could a child be born a natural with the ball at his feet, that strangers in parks and on beaches could start up a game with no words in common save the names of their clubs and their favourite players? A language of proper nouns, a lexicon of hero-worship and a grammar of unquestioning loyalty. At least with his job, the Young Man would be able to afford the instalments on his season ticket. Likewise the following season.

Because the Young Man had worked out that life wasn't about doing the things you wanted to do. It was about obligation, really – the obligation to keep going and accept responsibility for yourself. To live in the moment, yes, but not by discarding the future or the past. You had to hold it all in your mind at the same time, to let that tension be felt.

The Young Man only came to this realisation over the weekend. He was still only a young man, and there would be many more weekends like it. It didn't feel good to go back on his hopes and force himself to confront the world as it was, but then again, he guessed it wasn't supposed to.

33

TO STOP THEM BEING THROWN

LOSING WAS A HABIT; with the Finn officially ruled out for the rest of the season, it would be a hard one to break. And then, because it never rains, news broke online – on Friday night – that the Irishman had developed an ear infection. The Saturday paper confirmed it, and so Sunday's team sheet made for grim reading. The Norwegian was back in the eleven. The Kosovan would deputise up front, out of position. It seemed a lost cause, the last thing the Young Man needed.

It was embarrassing to admit, but ever since his girlfriend had left him, the Young Man's moods had become increasingly dependent on the football. It was pretty much the only thing he looked forward to: the next game, the next chance to arrest the team's run of losses, this poorly timed slide towards the relegation zone. He supposed he was lonely, was what it was. In his bleaker moments, he imagined everyone else was lonely too, that he was living through an epoch of isolation – only everyone else was too afraid to admit it. He pictured a community of the lonely, men and women like him who were unified only by their lack of connections, losing membership of this society as soon as they acknowledged and acted upon it, returning them to their default state of isolation and making them lonely once again.

The Young Man, when he was in this mindset, could believe that nobody knew anyone – really knew them. And come Sunday afternoon, he was just one of twenty-thousand lonely people, all dressed the same and singing the same songs, together but not together. He imagined it must be even worse for the Old Man; he had more to lose. He had been married for almost all his life, and he must have known that he was not far from either returning to nothing or returning to solitude. It threw the Young Man's experiences into perspective, made him think about the weight of all that time being released, decades coming down at once upon the Old Man to fill the space that death, loss, would inevitably make. Another man returned to loneliness, his default state.

Today, as usual, the Young Man emerged from the concourse to find the Old Man already in his seat. But the Old Man was staring at something, or someone, in the stand opposite. He was lost in thought, it seemed, an impenetrable look in his eyes. The Young Man approached him. He waited a second, and when the Old Man still did not acknowledge him, did not look away from that point in the distance, he cleared his throat.

The Old Man jolted back to himself. He stood to let the Young Man pass, a smile and a nod and the usual pleasantries. When they had said everything that needed saying about the

Finn's season-ending injury, they sat quietly for a while and waited for the stadium to fill up. The Young Man looked at the team sheet again, and then he listened as the announcer read the names and numbers over the stadium speakers. The Young Man shared a look with the Old Man. His look said they weren't safe yet and might never be, at this rate. Then he stood up for one last drink before kick-off.

Can I get you anything, he said.

No, said the Old Man. No thank you.

Are you sure?

The Old Man hesitated. He was without a jacket, and the hairs on his arms were standing up. His hands, veined like leaves, shook slightly in his lap.

Do they have pop? he eventually asked.

Yeah, said the Young Man. They have Coke. Do you want me to get you one?

No, thank you. The Old Man shook his head. After a brief pause he said, I'm fine.

The Old Man raised himself to his feet so the Young Man could pass. When he was alone again, he looked down to the pitch. The groundsmen were out, forking the playing surface at random – or so it seemed. The Old Man understood that the greenness of the turf was almost entirely artificial. Today's playing surfaces were a departure from the muddy pitches he had grown up with, but he supposed that was the point: things changed. Take this league: the envy of the footballing world, the toughest division anywhere. It was getting harder each year to survive; every point was a struggle, for a team like theirs. Today's game would be difficult.

The good news was that the Kosovan looked sharp in the

warm-up. It gave the Old Man a measure of hope. Even if the Kosovan was playing out of position, even if he was useless in front of goal, he would be better than nothing. The Old Man watched him doing one of his drills, lashing ball after ball into the empty net, the act of kicking refined beyond all sense and all humanity.

The Kosovan had the poise of a big cat. Although he rippled with muscle, he comported himself with such grace – such effortless, economical movement. He was something to watch, shaping his body to strike each ball in turn, jogging lightly on the spot between shots, flexing the taut sinews of his arms to get the blood moving faster, hotter. He curled another ball into the top corner. If only he could finish like that in the pressure of a match, the Old Man thought. The Kosovan reminded him of a Portuguese playmaker they had sold a few seasons ago; the Portuguese had been just as sure in his movement, but he was better than the Kosovan because he was a magician with a dead ball. It was a contrast to the Irishman, say. How the Irishman held himself, the clumsy and inelegant way he always seemed to be working against his own legs. Although none of that mattered, of course, when the ball was in the net.

The Kosovan's drill involved waiting on the arc, its white paint like a fictional border, while a coach passed balls at him. The Kosovan would strike each one with the side of his boot to send it curling between the posts – neatly into a top corner, more often than not. There was no goalkeeper to save his shots. The balls collected in the net until the coach paused the proceedings to retrieve the balls and start again. It was another exercise in the absurd, the Old Man thought. Then he realised this was true not just for the Kosovan and not just now but for every footballer, all the time.

Was not the ultimate figure of futility the footballer who scores a goal – an act, momentarily, of the highest importance – only for the game to reset immediately after? The Old Man was struck by the uselessness of trying to fight it, the sense of impotence which must have been common to many of the players. Take the forwards, uninvolved in the defensive effort, who can only stand and watch, hands on hips, as a goal goes in at the other end and all their efforts turn out to be for nothing. And the same process playing out game after game, year after year: the cycle of jubilation and the harshness of the reset, scoreboards returning to their inert state at the end of every match and the coming of the new season wiping away the residues of the old. The Old Man was deep in these thoughts when someone said his name.

He was wrenched back to the ground. He saw now that the stadium was almost full; it was loud and there were people all about him. The Kosovan was nowhere to be seen. Most likely, he was in the changing room, receiving his final instructions from the German. Kick-off was close. And there was the Young Man, lingering in the aisle as he waited for the Old Man to move out of the way, a bottle of cola – the caps removed – in each hand.

34

AGAINST THE RUN OF PLAY

It was hot in the Old Man's apartment. The balcony door was still without curtains, so the sunlight started coming in at lunchtime, heat building throughout the afternoon. The Old Man's wife was asleep in the armchair beside his. He could feel himself going, too. He was thirsty, and his mouth was dry. He knew he ought to get up and have a glass of water, but he didn't want to move. His bones were heavy. The football was on the television, and he was supposed to be watching. It was an important game. But he kept closing his eyes, and he had that awareness, now, that comes over a mind on the cusp of sleep. He caught his thoughts, appraised them – one by one, like a jeweller – and in their abstract notions he recognised that he was already more than halfway gone.

The Old Man felt himself slipping further away despite the noise from the television, which he had turned up to accommodate his wife's poor hearing. The chatter of the commentators cut crisply across his mind, although in his drowsy state it took him a second longer than it should have to process the meaning behind their words. The commentators were talking about the team's poor run of results, how they had played their way into the bottom three when it mattered most. They spoke over the sound of the fans, a martial cadence to the singing which surged from the stands, the intermittent beating of a dampened bass drum. They were talking about relegation, saying the club would go down if they didn't string together some results before the end of the season. Like so many games in this division, today's match would be tough. But if they were going to start putting up a fight, now was as good a time as any. These words, the voices of the commentators, seeped into the Old Man's subconscious, the barriers between him and the world dissolved by sleep. He felt as if he was the subject of the commentary, and all the babble was referring specifically to him. And then he was somewhere else.

In his dream he was at a fair, of sorts. The sun was bright overhead, and he could feel it all over his skin. It was loud, and there were bodies everywhere. *Now that's a decent effort on the turn, but ultimately, he's got to be hitting the target from that kind of distance. Yeah, I agree. It's a clean enough connection, but you really ought to test the keeper from there.* There was grass all around and a high fence which ran on one side, a copse of trees on the other. The Old Man realised where he was. He was in one of the fields behind his school, but now the wide expanse of grass was filled with stalls, like the market in the city. Some people he recognised and some he didn't were hawking their miscellaneous wares, competing for his attention. Everyone wanted him to buy something. A woman with a forgotten face beckoned him over, and he duly came to stand beneath the awning of her stall. Somehow, he found himself in the shade and in the glare of the sun at the same time, but this was not inconsistent with the logic of his dream, and he did not dwell on it. He focused instead on the woman, listening as she spoke a language he did not understand. It took a minute, but then he realised from her gestures that she was his mother. She held out a handful of trinkets: costume jewellery and metal chains and pendants with obscure engravings. He wanted to buy some, but he couldn't find his wallet. It wasn't in his pocket, where he always kept it. Where it should have been. *And that's the trouble, you see – right there; the centre-backs, when they step up like that, are always going to get exposed on the counter, what with both of them being so slow on the turn. There's nobody dropping back to cover that holding position and break up the play. And it's fair to say they've been lucky that the clinicality from the opposition strikers just hasn't been there today, or they might have found themselves a goal or two down already.* The Old Man was upset. It was important to him that he bought something from the woman who had become his mother. But he had no money and nothing to barter with. In the stall adjacent to his mother's, a man was selling live fish thrashing in their buckets, and on the other side was a florist whose bouquets were bunches of straw, each tied with a bright ribbon. His mother was imploring him to buy something – shouting in that obscure language, clearly distressed – but he couldn't. She was crying, and now he didn't recognise her any more. The gestures weren't the same. *And it's another gilt-edged chance which has gone begging! You've got to wonder if they're gonna regret not capitalising on this spell. Chance after chance here – it really is – but somehow, it's still nil-nil! You get the sense it just might not be their day today.* The flower seller called out to the Old Man, and the Old Man knew who she was even if he couldn't bring forth the name. He was trying to comfort the woman who had been his mother, but she flinched away when he reached out to her, gathering up her trinkets in jealous arms even as she cried for help, pulling back from his touch. Someone was thrusting a dry fistful of straw at him, and it tickled his face and scratched at the papery skin around his nose. The fishmonger was beating a fish against the counter to kill it. *And that could be a huge moment in the fight at the bottom of the table! Oh, it really could! It's a beautifully taken strike from a player who doesn't score many goals, and it came from a free-kick scenario just like the boys in the studio were talking about at the break. That really is against the run of play, but they don't care one bit! Just look at them – look at what that goal means to them. They'll take that any day, won't they? It's jubilation in the away dugout, it's a collector's item for the travelling fans, a first goal of the season for him, and it couldn't have come at a more crucial moment! But just look at those home supporters! They've been stunned into silence by that goal. The manager, too. And for him, the question is now: is there enough time left to get back in it and get something out of this game where they really have dominated the chances, you'd have to say?*

The Old Man was watching the television; the football was on. They had just gone one up. Replays showed the Kosovan celebrating with the travelling fans. He stood by the hoardings while the fans rushed down the steps to be closer to him. Some reached out and brushed their fingers against his shirt, and the Kosovan held out his arms and let them. The other players gathered around the Kosovan. The young Englishman gestured to his badge and then raised his hands as if exhorting the travellers to sing louder.

There was a face in the crowd, near the front. The Old Man knew who it was, but his dream had left him wary of certainties. The camera lingered, and he saw beyond doubt that it was the Young Man, going wild in the away end. The Old Man thought he ought to send him a text to say he had seen him on the television. Then he looked at the clock and saw how close they were to the whistle. His dream was already evaporating; it had taken on the substance of smoke, and in a second more he would lose his grip on it forever, forgetting that field where he had encountered, for the first time in many years, the visage of his mother. What was certain was the score of the game he was supposed to have been watching. They were winning. Three points would hoist them straight back out of the relegation zone. By itself, the victory would not be enough to keep them up, but it meant that safety, at last, was within reach. It also meant they held their own future in their hands, and at this late stage of the season, that was enough.

35

JUST A GAME

THE YOUNG MAN THOUGHT of her less, these days, but he still thought of her. He supposed that she must have been hurting too, although she was surely affected in different ways. He could not imagine her pining after him the way he had after her, restructuring her life to accommodate his absence the way he had tried to restructure his own life, tried to make sense of the wake of her, the space she had left behind. But now, for the first time, he conceded that the Old Man might have been right in offering his hopeful consolations. This intensity of feeling might not last forever.

The Young Man was still grateful, of course, for the time they had spent together. But more than that, he was grateful for the lessons she had taught him. Above all, and without really intending to, she had shown him how life really went – how people hurt the people they love, and they hurt strangers and they hurt themselves, sometimes. But the question of hurting and being hurt was mostly to do with love, the Young Man had learned, because the hurt usually needs a catalyst. Such was the way of things.

The Young Man, sitting in his usual seat on the terrace, pulled out his phone and, with reflexive muscle movements, unlocked it. He called up her profile without needing to search for it. He was thinking, still, about what he had lost, about the hurt behind her decision and the hurt after it. But even as these thoughts came, he recognised that what he was doing was not healthy. It would be far better to crowd out those echoes he felt whenever he saw her photos (her crying, shaking, in his bedroom, the moment when it had all started).

But it was easy to recognise when it was time to move on, and it was something else to actually do it. The trick was probably to do with being present, the Young Man supposed, and here was where the football could help – particularly after the surprise victory of the previous week, a crucial lift when the fans and the players had needed it most. Because it was also true that he had paid a not inconsiderable sum to be here, at the culmination of the season, almost, and he was behaving like one of those people whose attendance at the football he so often decried: seated, silent, looking at his phone. There were worse and less decorous modes of behaviour but only those to do with half-and-half scarves, filming penalties from the stands, and offering the consolation in the wake of defeat that it was only a game when, clearly, it was and always had been so much more than that. (His mother would no longer talk to him about football because he got so worked up about it; his father would no longer talk to him at all.)

How did they not see, these people? What was it they witnessed when they came, as tourists, to these secular temples? The army of supporters in their uniform, in one voice, having paid their tithes even though they were among those who could least afford it, performing rituals calcified over a lifetime and finding this one means of being with people rather than merely around them, some willing to bleed for the crest (no coincidence, of course, that it lies over the heart)... If it were just a game then things would not be this way. If it were just a game, nobody would go.

At that moment came a whistle, and the Young Man's attention returned to the pitch. The Englishman, the full-back, was being shown a yellow for dissent, having kicked away the ball after a free-kick was awarded against him. It was a stupid thing to do, barely fifteen minutes into the game. The German, on the edge of his technical area, threw up his arms in frustration. Getting booked like that bespoke a lack of maturity, and in this moment the Young Man had to remind himself that the Englishman – despite his professionalism and wealth and the total assuredness of his life – was immature, as all men are at that age. As the Young Man had been at that age and, in some ways, yet was.

Still, the Young Man turned to the Old Man, shaking his head, and said, That's a stupid yellow.

Yup, said the Old Man. He'll have to watch out for the rest of the game now.

They'll target him, the Young Man said. Just you watch.

I don't doubt it.

The game ticked on. Neither side was particularly good, in the context of the division, but the opposition was already mathematically safe, and from their perspective, the remaining fixtures were all friendlies. Sometimes it was a blessing to play against teams for whom the result was meaningless. Sometimes you could tell that the players were already on the beach, already checked-out, and it worked in your favour. Other times, it was a nightmare, the players delighting in the freedom of a meaningless match, a victory lap. There were days when timid, cautious footballers became uninhibited and expressive in ways they would never normally be. It meant you never knew what you were going to get, a match like today's, until it was too late. And today the opposition players seemed to float above the turf, unshackled after a season of restraint. Survival was their prize for a dour year of grinding out results, smashing and grabbing against bigger, better, richer clubs. Now it was their chance to play football, to ruin the parade. All elite athletes are bullies at heart, and today eleven of them had a chance to show the league how good they could be.

They were fearless, the opposition, playing like a weight had been lifted (which, of course, it had). They seemed to be playing their own game; their defenders danced past the Kosovan's feeble attempt at a high press and exposed voids in the midfield, where their squat and surprisingly agile playmaker kept confounding the Frenchman's attempts to get a foot in. More than once, their left-winger tied up the Englishman, turning his face red from embarrassment and exertion. The away fans cheered every pass. The yellows, on the other hand, had started to wear the pressure of the occasion on their faces. They telegraphed desperation in their shouts. The centre-halves were being run ragged, highlighting the desperate need to invest in the squad in the summer – in the event, of course, that they stayed up and had money to spend.

With half an hour gone, the Englishman was granted a chance to redeem himself for his earlier petulance. The opposition playmaker, spinning past the Frenchman's latest attempt at a tackle, played one of his long, diagonal balls, a pass that arced with the grace and precision of a cruise missile. It was headed straight for their right-winger, who had beaten the offside trap and found himself in more space than he could possibly need. The Dutchman made a mental calculation and sprinted from his line, scrambling to the edge of the box. But the Dutchman had got his maths wrong; he was too slow, and he ended up out of position, stranded in no-man's land with just one chance to stop the attack. The right-winger took the pass perfectly, killing the ball, and then he skipped closer to the byline, surprising the Dutchman (who was wrong-footed, having expected him to cut inside) and removing him from the equation entirely. There was the goal, and there was plenty of it to aim for. The angle was wide, but the net was unguarded. Quiet fell on the stadium; the away fans clenched their fists and opened their mouths and prepared to celebrate.

The right-winger took a fraction of a second to compose himself. He pulled the trigger, and from the moment it left his boot, the ball seemed destined to find the net. But then the Englishman was on the goal-line, scooping the ball clear with the top of his left boot before he himself went flying into the net, fingers lost in the webbing, as everyone else sprinted back into position. Only the right-winger stayed where he was. He dropped to a crouch and buried his face in his shirt, screaming his frustration. The Englishman had kept them in the game.

The Dutchman was presented with his own chance for

redemption late in the half when he stopped a one-on-one, making himself big and smothering the ball at the striker's boots. The centre-halves held up their hands in apology; no ball should slip between them like that, and yet it kept happening. It was a relief when the half-time whistle blew, the match somehow still level. The yellows had spent almost the whole half defending, and they had generated precious little at the other end – the Kosovan and his wasteful finishing had seen to that. It was one of those nil-nils where nobody believed it would end that way; it was a question of when, not if, the deadlock would be broken. Barring a major turnaround, the Englishman and the Dutchman and all the rest of them would end the day no safer than they had started it.

The whistle had not long blown for the restart when the day's headline was written. It was the Englishman, whose last-ditch clearance had been the talk of the concourse, praised in all corners of the ground by men young and old alike. But now the Englishman was the one who was out of position, rushing back towards his own goal with an opposition player between him and the ball. In a moment of desperation, he went to ground, knocking clear the ball only after he had gone through the attacker's legs, sending him flying to the turf and provoking an immediate uproar from the away fans. The home faithful shook their heads and set about muttering darkly to one another. They knew there was only one way this would end.

The linesman had been standing just a few yards from the challenge, and it seemed he had started waving his flag before the Englishman had even tracked back. A whistle, a shrill reprimand, rose into the air, piercing the awareness of both sets of fans. The referee – that wraith, that bastard, that killjoy – started walking over to the touchline, taking slow and measured steps and clearly enjoying his moment on the stage. They had a history with this referee, who had already spoiled one or two of their parties this season, and now he seemed to love how everyone had to wait for him, savouring the suspense. The Englishman hadn't got up from the tackle; he was lying on the turf, feigning injury and hoping for some sympathy from the referee, most likely. The man he had fouled was also still down, lying on the touchline with white paint streaked over his shorts and socks. A pair of physios were jogging over from the away dugout to assess him, this grown man playing dead because he felt he had been tackled unfairly in a game which meant nothing to him, toying with the fate of the club which belonged not just to the Young Man and the Old Man but to everyone else in this city as well.

Pathetic, said the Young Man. But the Old Man said nothing. He had seen it all before.

At last, the referee arrived at the scene. The away fans were calling for a second yellow, or even a straight red – they didn't care. Off! Off! Off! was the chant. The referee walked over to the Englishman, who was still on the floor. He stooped down to share some words with the teenager, and then he reached into his back pocket.

This particular referee exuded self-satisfaction, even from a great distance. It was easy for the Young Man to imagine his distant expression as he hoisted the card into the air, a second yellow. The away fans erupted, cheering this decision which was technically an act of clemency, two yellows amounting to just a one-game ban as opposed to a three-game ban for the dangerous conduct of a straight red. The referee returned the yellow card to his back pocket and produced the red card to accompany it. He wrote the Englishman's name and number on the back of the card, and then he held it aloft for everyone to see. Having ruined the game for the Young Man and his fellow supporters, the referee put away his card and his pen and turned his back on the Englishman, who despite being unhurt in the challenge was only now rising to his feet. The Englishman ambled towards the dugouts. He pulled off his shirt in disgust, accepting a conciliatory pat on the back from the German before heading down the tunnel.

The referee set about marking out the resulting free kick. He removed the canister from his belt and sprayed a dot of white foam where the dead ball would go. He added to this a single line, slashed against the turf ten yards away, to mark the distance of the wall. As he straightened up, having created his ephemeral border, a line which would fade after a minute or two, he tried to ignore the players crowding insensibly around him – as if he was going to change his decision now, as if he would call back the Englishman and make a show of brandishing the card in reverse, withdrawing it once more but only to cross his name and number off the back and return it symbolically to his pocket.

The Englishman was almost out of sight. He walked the final few paces down the tunnel without looking back. He had his shirt in his hands, balled up as if he had meant to throw it to the ground, and he looked faintly ridiculous in his GPS vest. It was early for a red card, particularly in a game of such importance.

That's us finished then, said the Old Man.

The Young Man looked to the scoreboard and its accompanying clock. There were still forty minutes to go, plus stoppages. No goals, but now the better side had the man advantage. A few people elsewhere on the terrace had stood up when the referee brandished his card, and now a small trickle of fans headed down the stairs, returning to the concourse. A quick pint to take the edge off the red card and the loss which it seemed to have made inevitable. The Young Man rose to join them.

Sorry, he said.

No problem, said the Old Man. He stood to let the Young Man pass.

Do you want anything? asked the Young Man.

The Old Man shook his head. He was still watching the pitch. It wasn't like the Young Man to miss any of the action. He wondered whether his heart wasn't in it today or if it was just the disappointment of the red, the near certainty of losing to a better team with more players and no pressure. The problem, he supposed, was that there was just too much at stake to enjoy the game.

But the Young Man's heart was in it, alright. He had too much heart, was the problem. He sipped at his pint in the concourse, watching first-half highlights on a television mounted on the wall. The screen was bothered on all sides by advertisements for companies that sponsored the club: a security contractor, an insurer, a local plastics manufacturer, a brand of coffee. A cheer surged from inside the stadium, but the Young Man didn't know why, and he didn't care to know. Probably just a wild shot, a stay of execution. He wondered, instead, what the Englishman was doing. He could imagine him in the changing room, raging about the referee even as he unstrapped his shinpads and threw them to the ground. A rage familiar to the Young Man and perhaps to all young men, the rage that comes when you love something and want it to be perfect, sadness turning to anger when you realise the world is not amenable to good things and never will be. (Rage that his father left, that she left, that there was nobody else.) And the frustration, also, that this – this result and this season and this sport – should matter so much to you and yet mean nothing to others, a world oblivious to a suffering you have, after all, wilfully chosen for yourself. The Young Man could see it now: the Englishman shirtless and taut with muscle and reeking of sweat and having probably condemned his team to another loss, risking relegation and all that entailed, enormous pressure for a man his age, a boy with a patchy beard and a professional contract... Try telling him it is just a game and see where that gets you.

36

SETTINGS AND PRIVACY

THE STAKES CONTINUED to mount, week on week. After the last time out – that demoralising, ten-man, second-half mauling – and with just three games to go, there was nowhere for any of the players to hide. One win, three more points, would guarantee safety, but now, when a single mistake or a flash of inspiration had the power to define a season, a career, it was impossible to predict how the players would react. That was the beauty of football. The German could have stayed up all night analysing tactics and formations, the men arranged on his whiteboard like so many chess pieces. He could have instructed every man in the precise rigours of how and when to defend and attack. He could have planned every detail of the transition and structured a month's worth of training sessions around one game. But as soon as that whistle blew, everything preceding it was erased. The players were human beings: they made stupid mistakes, they missed sitters and got themselves sent off. And yet, the inverse was also true. When it really mattered, even the most unassuming centre-half could score a forty-yard screamer in the dying seconds of a game, manna from heaven.

This was precisely how someone like the Young Man could become lost in his sport. How someone like the Old Man could sustain his interest over a lifetime, why he would only shrug if you told him the cumulative cost in pounds and hours of a lifetime of football fandom. It was not a flaw of the sport that ludicrous, unfair, unexpected things happened almost every match. In fact, the game was so beautiful because the players were fallible, because you could never predict what they'd do in the moment, when it really mattered. At least, it was easy to tell yourself that when your team was winning. And then there were days like today, when it was precisely the humanity of the players which made them so frustrating to watch.

So close to the end of the season, with so much hanging on the outcome of the final three games, the men in yellow might find new reserves of talent and courage, unearthing a steely competence nobody had ever reckoned with, surprising even themselves. They might win this game and, in doing so, save the season, validating all those months of denial and suffering – both theirs and the fans'. Or they might let the pressure get to them: crumbling from within, weakened by the knowledge that, had they only played better over the past few weeks, they wouldn't have wound up in such a precarious position, away from home against the runaway league leaders and desperate for a win or, at the very least, a hard-won point.

As it happened, they collapsed. They were clumsy in defence, where they missed the suspended Englishman, their backline hopelessly exposed without him. They let themselves get bullied in midfield, where the Frenchman had perhaps his worst game of the season. They were abysmal up front, where the Finn's clinical finishing or the Argentinian's close-quarters wizardry might have made the difference. In the absence of those heroes – one injured, one having betrayed them – they were shown up by the Irishman's inexperience and the Kosovan's ineptitude in front of goal. The fans were furious. They could tolerate losing – they might have tolerated relegation, even – but they would not stand for this, going down with a whimper.

Here we go again, said the stranger beside the Young Man, when the first goal went in. Fuck's sake, he added, when the second followed, not long after. He swore again at the third, shaking his head and grimacing at the field of play, the scene of a massacre. The Young Man said nothing.

Still, when the whistle came, the Young Man and the rest of the fans choked down their disappointment and applauded their team's meagre effort against a much bigger, much richer club. It was not worth booing them off, not so late in the season. The players needed their confidence intact for what remained of the run-in, and the fans knew it. The Young Man told himself he was only clapping the players because he wanted them to believe in the possibility of redemption, the following week. The next game was massive now. The final home game of the season, their best and penultimate chance to get the win they now desperately needed. Otherwise, they would have to rely on their rivals slipping up elsewhere. Otherwise, they would almost certainly go down.

After the whistle, the players scattered all over the field to shake the hands of their opponents and the rival manager.

Some players knew each other from their time in the league or from international duty, but the travelling players were mostly too despondent to chat. The exception was the Norwegian, who was making ready to swap his shirt with the most famous player on the opposing team. It wasn't clear what use a Ballon d'Or nominee would have for the Norwegian's shirt, but his would make for a nice souvenir for the Norwegian when he returned to his parent club in a few weeks' time.

The Norwegian had checked out a long time ago, the Young Man thought. He had practically arrived that way. The other players were better; most of them cared about the fate of the team, if only because relegation would look bad on their CVs. These players were coming over now to applaud the fans. The Norwegian stayed behind, talking to the opposition manager, perhaps audaciously sounding out his next move. The Young Man looked away from the Norwegian, focusing instead on the players who had been shepherded by the German into a neat rank, approaching the away block in this strange post-match formation, the line infantry of the modern age.

The players lingered for a minute or two to clap the fans after every game, but today the Young Man was struck by the surreality of this gesture, a rare recognition from the players that it was only the fans and their money that kept them in a job. This week the players had, in fact, paid out of their own wages to subsidise the supporters' tickets and travel to the game, an annual gesture which was more of a marketing gimmick than anything else. Still, it was better than nothing, and the Young Man reciprocated the applause to show, in his own small way, his gratitude for those of them who still gave a shit. He clapped even though he knew the German had to tell the players to do this, to drag their tired legs once more across the field and line up and applaud the fans. Although there were some exceptions, maybe, some players who didn't need to be told to hail the fabled twelfth man. The Dutchman was one of them. He was walking now beside the Irishman, both clapping. A moment later, the Irishman held up a hand in mute apology for a poor game. The fans loved to see that, a player taking responsibility. They clapped back, louder than before.

The Dutchman put an arm around the Irishman's shoulder. He leaned close to say something over the noise of the stadium. The Young Man could only guess what the Dutchman was saying to his young teammate. Was he offering paternal assurance, words of courage and a promise that everything would be okay come the end of the season? Or perhaps the Dutchman was just sharing a joke, or a stock tip. The Young Man would never know, although he imagined the Dutchman was not the type to shy away from the Irishman's worries. He could not imagine the Dutchman quitting a game before either side had mated the other, the rooks still in their corners and the pawns unmoved, a gambit of abandonment.

Soon the players were done with their post-match obligations and were heading for the tunnel, a cold bath and a massage and a debrief to follow. The Young Man made for the steps, no team consolation for him and no rub for his aching foot. Instead, he steeled himself for the long journey back. It was slow going down the concrete stairwell, an interminable distance to the designated gate for away fans and the coach on which they had arrived. Men and women (but mostly men) in yellow jerseys and stylised away strips pressed around him. One of the few women brushed her bare arm against his, and his heart quickened, hairs rising at the frisson of human contact. Nobody had touched him, skin-on-skin, since his girlfriend; already, that sensation – and those that accompanied it – had been relegated largely to the world of his imagination.

The woman who had nudged him apologised and turned back to her conversation. She was talking to two men – brothers, perhaps – about next week's game. Most of the fans travelled with family or friends. After a win there was usually singing as they left the ground.

There would be no singing today. Instead, there was just sombre speculation about the next fixture. They were saying it was a must-win; the players had to treat it like a cup final. If they were going to stay up, it would be next week when they did it: at home, with the Englishman back. Both remaining games were against good teams, but strange things happened this late in the season and they were not down until they were down. Soon the stairs levelled out, and the stream of fans emerged into the open. Home beckoned.

As soon as the Young Man had found his seat on the coach, he pulled out his phone and connected his headphones. He was already dreading Monday morning – dreading another five days of work, knowing he'd end up utterly crushed if they lost the match at the end of it – and this weekend wasn't even close to being over.

The coach started moving. There was conversation behind him, an analysis of the likely players they'd keep and lose if they went down, but the Young Man distracted himself by turning up his music and opening social media. The first post on his feed was a news story, a timeline of the accusations (now all dropped, amid talk of more settlements and fresh NDAs) against the league's most famous footballer. The Young Man pressed the search bar and followed the first suggestion. The algorithms which governed his life had discerned a great deal about what sort of man he was, and yet he still wasn't quite ready to clear his search history and erase his data. It was easier to find her profile this way.

She had posted an update since kick-off. A bright new tile in the mosaic of her life, a fiction of comfort and completeness which she rigorously curated and edited before presenting herself to the world. To look at her from without, you would assume she was happy. That was always how she seemed in her pictures, anyway. Some fifty people had liked this latest photo. It was her with her hair down. She was in one of the coastal towns within striking distance of the city. She was wearing a man's jumper. He recognised the pier which loomed in the background of the shot, and there was a tag above the image which confirmed where the photo had been taken. He looked through more of her recent posts, but he had seen them all before. There were no new comments.

He changed to another app and saw that she had been active in the last five minutes. If he were to write a message, expressing how he felt, she would probably see it straight away. She might even reply. But he didn't want to do that. Instead, he changed apps again and slipped down a feed of generational angst, updates from the undulating, urbanised front lines of the war and, of greater interest to him, transfer speculation about the coming off-season. Because the apps he used were free, he was the product. He knew this, but it did not bother him enough to stop using them.

She was online now. There was another like on her latest

post. People were saying that the Englishman would be sold to a major club on the continent, that it was immoral to have children because the planet was dying. He closed his eyes against the noise and turned up the music again, almost as loud as it would go. He was still listening to his father's old rock albums, recognising as he did that he himself was like a broken record.

The Young Man leaned his head against the window. He could feel, deep in the space inside his skull, the vibrations of the road. These vibrations rose, like the aftershocks of an earthquake, through the tempered glass and came directly into his thoughts. He imagined scenes of devastation, great fissures in the asphalt and buildings slipping, crumbling like diseased bones and falling into his path. Telegraph poles strewn against the verge: wires knotted, frayed and burning. And amid that ruin, the Young Man anticipated the still life of a breakdown on the hard shoulder: a family of three pulled over with their hazards flashing, lights lost to the flickering of a thousand fires. He imagined how they would be oblivious to the chaos around them, absorbed utterly in their own small drama, their search for food and water and an emergency phone, the stranded boy deep in his own search for paternal reassurance. The world was ending, and all he needed was a few words of courage and a promise that everything would be okay, come the end of the season.

The Young Man could picture this scene so clearly and intently that he soon took his own place within it, experiencing the aftermath of the breakdown simultaneously from the perspective of the father and the son until he became, instead, the vibrations themselves, the juddering sensation beneath all these thoughts. He looked out for such a scene as the coach drove on. Any second now, he expected to come across that stricken family – that smallest of tribes, unified against the rage and indifference of the world beyond – but of course, he never did.

On the seat behind him, a man was talking to his son, pointing out the name of their city on a passing road sign, commenting on how far they had yet to travel. The Young Man heard the words, felt the love behind them, even over the strains of his father's music, soft female vocals and crisp drums and the tame purr of an electric guitar. The Young Man closed his eyes, and then he held the volume button on his phone, turning the music all the way up – so loud that it overtook even the vibrations, the echoes, the hopes he would forever associate with the roadside and the day's humiliating defeat so that he was left with just the music: the songs his father had listened to, once, when he was the Young Man's age, and perhaps listened to still.

37

NOTHING LEFT IN HIM

With five minutes to go and one goal in it, a fresh nervousness was rising among the fans. Almost as soon as the stadium clock ticked over to eighty-five minutes – the scoreboard beside it showing a slender lead for the home team – a shrill whistle came from the terrace, somewhere over the Young Man's shoulder. More people joined in, whistling with their mouths because it was better than just waiting, hoping. Then, as the clock ticked on, the sound seemed to replicate until there were hundreds of whistles, thousands, cascading from the stands, originating in every corner of the ground. The fans were trying to induce the referee to blow early, not that he ever would. Still, the whistling intensified with every minute, and after ninety had passed, the tension was so great that being in the stadium (every seat sold, the highest attendance of the season) felt like being trapped in an enormous teakettle, steam rising all around and the deafening sound of screeching and the sense that the place was ready to explode, any moment now.

Whenever a home player made a tackle, with every block and clearance and successful interception, the fans cheered – shouts of encouragement drowning even the whistling. If you looked closely, the very air above the pitch seemed to be crackling, shimmering like a heat haze with all that nervous energy. When the board went up saying there would be four minutes of added time, there were boos, and a furious edge glinted suddenly in the sunlight, something which had been hidden beneath the atmosphere of hope and maybe even piety. Someone in the row behind the Young Man and the Old Man asked whether the referee had come on the same coach as the away team.

Blow the fucking whistle! another man shouted.

It was May, deep into the business end of the season. In truth, there was barely any season left, and in four minutes' time the fans would know whether they would look back on this year, in the days to come, with fondness or regret. The long summer always granted plenty of time for reflection. This awareness fed into the mounting desperation in the stands, the hope that all would be well and that the aggregate score of all those Saturday afternoons would amount to something. All those fans wanted, really, was an achievement they might be able to share. A sense of security to carry them through the barren summer until the table was reset, alphabetised with everyone on zero points, and they started all over again, thirty-eight more games in which the players might prove themselves anew. But they had to get there first. They had to win this game to make sure they'd stay up.

The Young Man and the Old Man shared a look. It was an expression of joy and hope and surprise and more than a little fear: joy at the one-goal lead the Irishman had won them; hope that the lead would hold for just three more minutes; surprise that on his return from suspension, the Englishman had produced not only a defensive masterclass but also supplied the cross the Irishman had nodded in, unmarked, at the back post; and fear that they would concede late, when it hurt most, and throw it all away. It was clear to both men: the way they had been playing recently, this game wasn't over until it was over. But if this win held – if they actually pulled it off – then they would have everything they needed. And now mathematical certainty was just two minutes away, although a single miskick, one misplaced pass, could yet damn them – not only dropping them into the relegation zone but sealing off their most likely escape route, condemning players and fans alike. Although, of course, they were not alike.

All the players had clauses in their contracts which triggered wage deductions if they were relegated. Some stood to lose half their income at a stroke, but they would still be able to travel in the off-season and get their cars wrapped at the garage out of town. Still, many would want to find a different club if that happened. Their being under contract meant only that the club could demand a bigger transfer fee when they inevitably moved on. It was really the non-playing staff who were most affected: the physios and the chefs and the cleaners. Some had termination clauses if they went down. And you had to situate these events in their proper context: living was becoming more expensive all the time. Everywhere, across the country, across what remained of the Western world, things were breaking and going wrong. But staying up was all that mattered to the people who worked for the club and the fans who propped it up, who were brave enough to dream that this final minute might pass without event.

Neither the Old Man nor the Young Man had expected to become quite so invested in this season; they had not bargained that so much else in their lives would change and worsen since that first game and that this one constant would, in the absence of much else, assume an even greater importance. It was not healthy, but their emotional wellbeing depended on the outcome of these final seconds. Their place in the league was one more thing they couldn't bear to have taken from them, and they were not alone in the stadium in feeling that way. And so it was natural that the fans wanted to play their part, no matter how small. They wanted to tell themselves, when they looked back on this day, that theirs had been one of the voices which dragged the team over the line. They wanted to believe, for one period of stoppage time, that they really were the twelfth man, that this victory would be as much theirs as their players'. See, then, the Old Man putting two fingers to his chapped lips and whistling; see the Young Man looking to the clock and then doing the same. See their legs jigging, hands shaking. Hear how they sing for courage, for the reassurance that they are not alone in caring too much about this thing which ought not to matter. How the echo of their song proves that others feel the same as them.

The Englishman cleared the ball deep into one of the stands, conceding a throw-in but keeping danger at bay for a few more seconds. A great cheer went up, and then the whistling intensified. The ball was in the hands of the supporters now, and they threw it among themselves, ever higher and further from the pitch, hoping to run down the clock as much as they could. An opposition player, waiting to throw it in, was standing on the touchline with his hands on his hips and mud streaked down the sides of his socks, watching as the ball was carried ever further from the field of play. Maybe half a minute was killed in this way before a new ball was reluctantly handed over by a partisan ball-boy and play resumed. As soon as the throw-in had been taken, the missing ball was returned to the field, stopping play for a few seconds more. The referee kept looking at his watch. Everyone was standing now, thinking he was about to blow, but he didn't. The Old Man felt a nudge from the Young Man. He was saying something, but the words weren't getting through. The Old Man was too absorbed in the action. He was watching not the ball but the referee, willing him to blow. Still play continued: another attack, another clearance.

The Old Man had tried to work out all the permutations earlier that morning. He had been using the league table in the paper, which was already out of date but which showed clearly that nothing less than three points would be enough. He had let the numbers swim before his eyes – figures in cheap ink showing, for all twenty clubs, how many games they had played, how many points they had won, goals for, goals against, goal difference – but then his wife had said something to bring him back, something about how he had been a fool to move her here, across the city, and expect her to keep her mind with just him for company. And they still needed curtains; he kept saying he would take care of it, but he never did. Since when had he been so bloody useless?

The Old Man had been so surprised to hear his wife speaking like that that he hadn't been able to reply. She was becoming sharper with him, he thought. It worried him. After the game, he would sit down with her and talk about what she needed and maybe open up that old can of worms about moving again, finding somewhere she liked. But the worst thing was that she was just as likely to have forgotten her complaints by the time he was back, kissing him on the cheek if she had listened to their win on the wireless, offering a commiseration if they lost and saying that the club had been going downhill for a while now anyway, hadn't it? The Old Man knew he would gladly parcel out any other piece of himself before he gave up his mind, and he was so lost to these dark thoughts that he did not notice the Young Man looking at him, asking if he was okay.

The Young Man nudged the Old Man again, and this time he came back: the whistles like a demonic chorus, the black of the referee's uniform, in which the Old Man had become lost, the scoreboard with one goal for the home team and none for the visitors. The opposition had the ball, but every home player was behind it, defending, prepared to give anything, everything, to protect their lead. It was just as well that the Norwegian was watching from the bench because he would not have been much good in such a scenario. It was time for the gladiators, this late and with so much at stake.

There can't be long left now, said the Young Man. Seconds, if that.

The Old Man nodded. He counted in his head: one, two, three. The opposition still had the ball, but they couldn't get through. The Irishman pushed up, forcing a backwards pass, and the fans cheered like they had scored. The referee looked once more at his watch and raised his whistle to his lips. One, two, three blasts of the whistle, and it was over.

Pandemonium gripped the terrace, fans shouting and laughing and triumphant music coming, already, from the speakers. Down below, many of the players dropped to their knees, weakened by relief, while the German punched the air and ran to the centre circle, mobbed by his backroom team and by the subs. His cap went flying off in his elation, although he did not seem to notice.

The Old Man, in the midst of the youthful jubilation which defined the terrace on days like these, reached out and grabbed the Young Man's arm. He had a surprising strength in his grip, and the Young Man was shocked at the desperation behind such force. His fingernails were also slightly too long, so that the Young Man felt their crescents against his skin, but it was a happy moment, and the Young Man was beaming as he turned to the Old Man and said, We fucking did it!

We did it! the Old Man responded, grinning, letting go now so that he might clap his hands. He appeared, for the first time all season, perfectly steady on his feet, wholly assured in his own body. Such was the revitalising tonic of victory; both men felt lighter, free of all the pains that had built up over the season. They did not stop for a second to consider the fans who would be condemned by their success, the club that would be relegated in place of their own. It had all been worth it; that was what mattered.

Cheers were ringing all around, and a chorus of the club song started up, scored by the drum at the back of the terrace. The players, mostly, were still on the floor, some laughing and cheering and some with their heads in their hands, disbelieving. The German picked his way between his men, patting backs and rubbing heads and shaking hands, a picture of relief. When the German reached the Irishman, he pulled the young striker to his feet, and although the Young Man could not possibly hear what the German was saying, he knew he would be encouraging the Irishman to enjoy this moment, his moment. He had earned it, as they all had.

The Englishman was lying on his back, making sure everyone could see that he had nothing left in him. Only the Norwegian and the Dutchman appeared full of life. The former because he didn't really care and never had; he was shaking hands and talking to a player on the other team. The Dutchman, meanwhile, was bigging it up with the fans behind the goal, celebrating with the working men and women of this city, strangers with whom he shared a dream and in whom he recognised fragments of himself, how he might have turned out if he hadn't been funnelled through an elite academy as a child, scouted and coached and moulded into a professional footballer, a millionaire. The fans loved the Dutchman because they too could recognise themselves in him, and now they started singing his name. He slapped one of his oversize gloves against his chest, where the crest was, beaming so brightly the Young Man could see his artificially whitened teeth from all the way back on the terrace. Then the Dutchman unstrapped his gloves and tossed them into the stand, one after the other. He did the same with his shinpads. The travelling players seemed to have disappeared already; the away fans were silent, melting away from the ground and the awareness of both the Young Man and the Old Man.

The Englishman was up at last and making his way over to

the stand opposite theirs. Someone in the front row was holding up a sign, and the Englishman was taking off his shirt as he walked. The Frenchman was clapping the sky; the Kosovan had a phone in his hand and appeared to be filming the scenes of jubilation taking place all around the ground. The Finn, with one foot in a boot and a crutch in each hand, had even limped over from the dugout to join in the celebrations. The German broke off a display of backslapping with his assistant manager to greet the Finn, pulling him into a hug. They were safe, and so was he.

The Old Man smiled and turned to the Young Man. That's a turn-up for the books, he said. One game spare, as well.

I know, said the Young Man, beaming. He ran a hand through his hair; he felt wild, feral, sweaty from all the nervousness and the celebrations. But he was as happy as he had been all season. I can't believe it, he said, raising his voice over the din of the stadium. We've actually done it.

Never doubted it for a second, said the Old Man. He winked.

The Young Man laughed. Speak for yourself, he said.

The two men were quiet for a moment, absorbing the joy of the stadium, letting the party atmosphere settle. A stranger reached forward and shook both of their hands. The drum started up again somewhere behind them: a new rhythm, a beat reserved for victory.

Then the Old Man said, You know, you should come over for a beer some time. So we can celebrate properly.

The Young Man raised his eyebrows. Really?

Of course, said the Old Man. These days I don't drink, myself, but it would be no trouble to get some beers from the shop, if you tell me what kind you like.

I'm not fussy, said the Young Man, smiling.

I thought as much. Well. You can come over any time. You know how to reach me.

Thank you, said the Young Man. But even then, as he looked into the slowly blinking eyes of the Old Man – the skin loose and the off-whites run through with vessels like red string – he knew he would never really go. Which was why, amid the depersonalising chaos of the stadium, that afternoon at the end of the season, it had been so kind of the Old Man to offer.

THE LONG SUMMER

IT WAS THE FINAL FIXTURE of the season, and now they were finally safe, the Young Man hoped he might be able to enjoy it. He had already set in motion the process of renewing his season ticket for next year, prices frozen to help with the cost of living, but he wasn't sure whether he'd commit again to so many away games. Maybe he would go to some, the closer ones. But he probably wouldn't recreate this feat: following the team to almost every fixture, covering so many miles, viewing so many white-on-green road signs from within the interchangeable interior of the supporters' coach. It was time-consuming and expensive, and it was nice to think of this final game as an epilogue, a conclusion to all those hours on the road in which he always seemed to end up lost, too deep for comfort, in his own anxieties.

The previous week, after the celebrations had died down,

the Young Man had asked the Old Man if he too was going to renew his ticket.

I don't know, the Old Man had said. It's an expensive hobby.

Tell me about it, said the Young Man. He knew well that it was a question of trade-offs; he had been able to afford his own ticket by foregoing international holidays, cutting back on train journeys and meals out. He suspected, however, that the Old Man's reluctance had less to do with the cost and more to do with his wife. The Old Man did not like to leave her alone, the Young Man had gathered. Her health wasn't good, and she was only likely to get worse. Perhaps the Old Man couldn't enjoy the games while he was worrying about her. The Young Man knew he had been the same with his girlfriend. And then he had realised: that was the first time he had thought about her all day. Football retained its power to distract, after all.

But this was a new week, one last game before the long summer and perhaps the Young Man's last away game for a long time. He would not miss these journeys – the early starts and the forced camaraderie among the travelling fans – but it had been something to see all those stadiums, to note the differences between each one: starkly evident, given the general unity of the form. The shapes of the grounds and the atmospheres they cultivated, the interaction of the tangible and intangible factors that made each one unique. The flavour of the crowds. Subtle alterations to the dimensions of the pitch, smaller for the lesser clubs and larger for the more technical sides. It seemed you could keep arranging however many thousand seats around a rectangle of uniformly marked turf, repeating the exercise into infinity, and come up with a different design each time.

These thoughts lifted the Young Man on his long journey,

kindled his anticipation for a fixture which didn't really mean anything to either side, a dead rubber. It was a wonderful thing to have secured safety at home, in front of their own fans, and not least because the fixture computer had been so unkind. Not only were they away from home on the final day of the season, but they were away on the other side of the country, against a top-half team. It seemed the fixture computer was often unkind to the smaller clubs. The bigger clubs did well out of it. It was like everything else, in that respect. But that was just the way things were going with the game, and there wasn't anything the Young Man could do about it. Short of refusing to attend, of course, but that would be much too drastic a protest – like threatening to end all of civilisation because you didn't agree which flag belonged with which stretch of land, where the lines ought to be drawn on other people's maps.

The Young Man did not know what he would do with his weekends after this one. The real game was played at club level, and international football was a poor substitute. The Young Man would have to find another way to spend his time off. It would be a long and hot summer, he knew.

He thought of the heat as an isolating force, in its way, because it exposed the stronger bonds of others. Social rituals were brought into the open whenever the sun persisted for more than a couple of days, and he knew the greens of his city would soon fill with children and their parents. The market would become a press of bodies. The cathedral would be remade into a sanctuary from the heat. The Young Man could feel the cool air of the churches already, footsteps reverberating on the flagstones and the interiors so dingy, after the light outside, that your eyes need a few seconds to adjust. These spaces crowded already with shade-seekers, mobs intruding on his thoughts, forcing him to confront everything he lacked.

But at least the team was safe. And at least he was not alone in understanding the significance of such an outcome, the joy of which was not individually portioned like so much in life but heaped right there in the stands for the supporters to share. The Old Man would agree with him, he knew. All the other fans, too. Theirs was an understanding common to the supporters of all clubs, in fact – perhaps even to fans of other sports. This was football as a protest against the atomisation of society, a meek means of fighting back but one which worked, often enough, for ninety minutes at a time. You could forget a lot in ninety minutes. You could discover a lot about yourself, too.

And the joy of survival – the relief which lightened the step and reminded young men that the world could still be beautiful, and that some of that beauty was yours to have – would last all summer before the gains of the past year were wiped away and the new season started from zero. It was this thought to which the Young Man returned as he watched the final game, his eyes drawn to the crisp white of the touchline and the boundaries it formed: fans on one side, players on the other. When they went one up, he felt an arm around his shoulder, a face he didn't recognise. And as the figure of the Irishman, the goalscorer, ran the length of the pitch to celebrate with the travelling fans, the Young Man gave himself over to the absurd diorama below, reaching out for the stranger beside him as the announcer grudgingly read out the name and number of the young Irishman, the minute of the goal.

ACKNOWLEDGEMENTS

THESE ACKNOWLEDGEMENTS can only start and end with my partner, Emily: an astute reader of early drafts, a cover-design genius and a source of support and encouragement at all the times when I have needed it most. Nobody has done more than her to shape me or my work, nor has anyone had to endure so much of my moaning and whining about a path I willingly chose for myself.

When I had the idea for *Season*, Emily was the first person I discussed it with, and with every subsequent draft she gave me valuable feedback and encouragement. I know that she has also made many sacrifices on my behalf, suffering me and my art when it would have been the easiest thing in the world to suggest that maybe I ought to just get a real job or consider toning down my aspirations. Instead, I am ludicrously lucky to have found a partner who not only shares my ambitions but who pushes me to want more for myself and sustains me with her belief. Emily, you're a worldie.

I wrote much of *Season* in the summer of 2022, but it wasn't until I became involved with the National Centre for Writing that the first draft developed into something worth reading. As part of NCW's brilliant Escalator Talent Development Programme, I worked with Michael Donkor, who mentored me over the best part of a year as I developed, rewrote and edited the book. As well as being a staggeringly insightful editor and an enthusiastic advocate for fellow writers, Michael is an all-round joy to work with and a great person to know. He immediately recognised what I was trying to do with *Season*, and his guidance helped me tease out what mattered and cut the rest. In the process, he became one of my most energetic and valued supporters, and it was his insight and advice which helped me turn the early drafts of *Season* from Sunday League to Semi-Pro. Michael, I'm very grateful for the assist.

I'm also very grateful to all the staff and supporters of the National Centre for Writing. The backing of this brilliant literary institution hastened me on the path to publication, introduced me to some great people, and helped shape my career. Dragon Hall will always feel like home turf.

I'm also lucky to have friends in Norwich – in both the writing world and the real world – who have supported me with kind words and encouragement, read the novel, and generally helped me on the way to publication. Ashley Hickson-Lovence was another of *Season*'s earliest advocates. He's a fantastic writer and an even better man, and I'm so grateful to have him on my team. Ashley, for a United fan, you're alright.

I'm also hugely grateful to Nick Padamsee and Aga

Maciejewska: fellow Norwich fans and valued supporters of my work. It seems very fitting that when I received the offer to publish *Season*, Nick and Aga were among the first people I told – and it is even more fitting that our conversation should have taken place in the terrace bar at Carrow Road. Thank you for your friendship and your belief. It has been wonderful to celebrate goals and successes with you both over the past year or so, and I hope there are many more to come. OTBC.

I have another Norwich-supporting writer to thank in the form of David Taylor. David read *Season* and offered a great deal of valuable support and advice before I had even found a publisher. I'm grateful to have the backing of a true legend of the writing game.

I'm also grateful to Ferdia Lennon – another great Norwich-based writer and someone who has been enthusiastic and supportive whenever the book has come up in conversation. A good laugh and a glorious guy.

This book would probably never have been published without the efforts of my agent, Tom Cull. Having worked together on various non-fiction projects in the past, I was delighted that Tom saw the potential in *Season* and chose to take a long shot on my behalf. I'm grateful to Tom for his belief and for all his hard work behind the scenes. Thanks for representing me with the industry and tireless enthusiasm of a box-to-box midfielder and for having found the perfect publisher for this book.

On that note, I'm very grateful to Dan Hiscocks and the team at Eye Books. They may be a small outfit, but their work is of top-flight quality, and they are consistent over-achievers in a league dominated by a few big-spending giants. Publishing needs more plucky indies like Eye and their fiction imprint

Lightning, and I'm pleased to say I have greatly enjoyed working with them. Thanks are also due to Ifan Bates, for designing a fantastic cover which perfectly captures the essence of *Season,* to Clio Mitchell, for her work on the typeset, and to Simon Edge, my editor, who approached this novel with clarity of vision and a reassuringly comprehensive understanding of what *Season* is and ought to be about. It's fair to say that Simon completely got me and my novel from the very beginning, and *Season* is a much better book for all his astute, incisive suggestions. Thanks, Simon.

Away from publishing, I'm grateful also to my family: my parents, obviously, as well as Ollie and Janey. Thank you for the support and encouragement in all its forms over so many years.

On that note, I'm also grateful to Tim, Amanda and Laura Dinsmore, who have always been incredibly supportive of me and my work and in whose house I was staying when I first started working on *Season.*

Thank you, also, to all the other friends and members of my wider family who helped or encouraged me along the way. This includes everyone who has shown an interest in my work, read any of my drafts, or with whom I have shared a good conversation about literature or, in this case, football.

I'm grateful to more people than you could fit in a dressing room – perhaps more than you could fit in an entire stadium – but as a non-exhaustive list, I'd like to place on record my thanks to: David and Ros Angel; Lauren Windle; Chico, Dermot, Rohan, Ollie and the rest of the LSE gang; Martin Hanson; Simon Hayes; and Ellie Bunn and Jordan Bowman.

As with any major creative project, there are times along the way when writing a novel seems like an impossibly long and almost certainly fruitless endeavour. At times like those, the smallest crumbs of validation can nourish the spirit. Thanks, everyone. Let's be having you.

As ridiculous as it may sound, I'd also like to thank everyone connected with Norwich City Football Club. In various ways, the club has been a constant for me since my early childhood, and the Canaries have been the source of much joy and pride at even the most difficult times of my life. Grant Holt was the one player whose story and spirit made me fall in love with football; thanks are due to him for banging in so many vital goals over the years and for inspiring in me a strange and affirming affection for our national sport – without which I would never have written this book.

And just before the final whistle blows, I must return to where I started and thank Emily once more. Without her, I don't know where I'd be, and *Season* would probably still be an idea in my head. Like Harry Kane or James Maddison, this project has been a true Norwich/Tottenham collaboration, and like everything good in my life, there's a lot of Emily in this book. Ems, you are the most beautiful person. I love our life together. Thank you.

Also from Lightning

The Mating Habits of Stags
Ray Robinson
Shortlisted for the Portico Prize 2020

Midwinter. As former farmhand Jake, a widower in his seventies, wanders the moors of North Yorkshire trying to evade capture, we learn of the events of his past: the wife he loved and lost, their child he knows cannot be his, and the deep-seated need for revenge that manifests itself in a moment of violence.

On the coast, Jake's friend, Sheila, receives the devastating news. The aftermath of Jake's actions, and what it brings to the surface, will change her life forever. But how will she react when he turns up at her door?

The Mating Habits of Stags is a journey through a life of guilt and things unsaid. As beauty and tenderness blend with violence, Robinson subtly explores love and loss in a language that both bruises and heals.

Poetic and powerfully brutal. A one-off
The Times

A wonderfully empathetic account...full of candour, lyricism and compassion
The Spectator

Extraordinary…gets under the skin from the first paragraph. A bittersweet and starkly beautiful tale that lingers long in the memory
Yorkshire Post

A taut, spare story of survival that turns on its heel to become something altogether braver, rarer and more precious
Melissa Harrison

If you have enjoyed *Season*, do please help us spread the word – by putting a review online; by posting something on social media; or in the old-fashioned way by simply telling your friends or family about it.

Book publishing is a very competitive business these days, in a saturated market, and small independent publishers such as ourselves are often crowded out by the big houses. Support from readers like you can make all the difference to a book's success.

Many thanks.

Dan Hiscocks
Publisher, Eye Books